Pain of Innocence

Pain of Innocence

By

Lorene Wingard

Illustrated by

Julie Caffee

Ozark Publishing, Inc.
P.O. Box 228
Prairie Grove, AR 72753

Library of Congress cataloging-in-publication data

Wingard, Lorene, 1925-
    Pain of innocence / by Lorene Wingard ; illustrated by
Julie Caffee.
      p.   cm.
    ISBN 1-56763-297-1 (alk. paper). — ISBN
1-56763-298-X (pbk. : alk. paper)
    I. Title.
    PS3572.I96P35   1997
    813'.54—DC20   96-42247
                                                              CIP

Printed in the United States of America

iv

For Mary

Prologue

The sharp clanging sounds and the pungent odors of alcohol and the medicines brought my mind slowly into focus. I could hear hurried footsteps and muffled voices coming from the hallway. I must be in a hospital. Somewhere in the distance I could hear cars passing and an occasional siren leaving an eerie sound drifting in the air. My body felt numb and tired, oh so tired. I wanted to open my eyes, but my eyelids were too heavy, and I didn't have the strength even to try.

I could still see all the little people (they must have been doctors and nurses) in their drab-green suits and masks. I felt excruciating pain, and there was blood. I was on a cart, and someone was pushing me fast down the corridor and people were running. I heard them say that we were headed for the delivery room, but what for? What was I going to deliver? A calm, soothing voice kept saying, "push," then "no, don't push," and I hurt. I wanted to get it out, whatever it was, to stop the pain. I felt hands pushing and pulling and heard voices, and Mom was there. I heard the doctor say this was a seven-month baby. It couldn't be mine. I couldn't be seven months pregnant. I had the bloody curse every month. Who could have told them that this baby was mine? Was someone punishing me? There was more pain and an urgent voice commanding me not to push, the cord was around the baby's neck. I pushed anyway. I couldn't help it. I was being torn apart. God, help me! Finally I got rid of it, and the pain let up for a minute. Oh thank You, God. What did he say? A baby girl, but too small, and someone was having to breathe for her. The doctor said he was sewing me back up. My mother sews, you know. She makes almost all of my clothes. I'll bet her serger would have done a real good job.

I'm so tired, I have to go to sleep. I don't want to dream anymore. I don't like these kinds of dreams. The people are all so little. Tomorrow, maybe tomorrow, I can wake up. Oh my! I think I have a test tomorrow.

Chapter 1

The night had been long and tiring for nurse Irene Morgan. Her shift had had not one, but two emergency deliveries. Her feet ached, and her back and shoulders felt like a hot poker was stabbing up and down. At age forty-eight, she sometimes felt like she was at least a hundred. She had seen so much suffering and pain, and nothing ever seemed fair. She had started her career some twenty-five years ago, full of dreams and illusions of how she would save all the people. She had hardened in the ensuing years and had finally faced up to the fact that her job was often ugly and futile. Oh, she still loved her work, and there were bright days, but she had come to realize that only God had the ultimate say in the living and dying.

Tonight had been another strain. Two baby girls, born a couple of hours apart, both premature, weighing under three pounds each, and both in bad shape. Not too much hope for either of them. For the Lamberts, Joan and Paul, this was their last chance. They had tried for years to conceive but to no avail. At last after some corrective treatments, Joan finally got pregnant. They were delighted and had looked so happily toward the day when they would at last be parents. Joan was thirty-six, and she had been so careful all during her pregnancy. Even with all her precautions, she couldn't carry the baby full term.

The other child was the product of an unwed teenage college student, Leslie, and there was no telling who the father was. She was hardly more than a baby herself and scared. Irene felt sorry for her. She didn't even seem to know that she was pregnant, and her mother was in a state of shock. The girl's father hadn't showed up yet. No telling what would happen to that tiny being if she lived. This was an unexpected and unwanted baby. No, things weren't fair. The Lamberts were such a nice couple.

Well, all Irene could do was to take care of the little tykes as best she could until her relief came. Of all mornings her replacement would have to be late! Irene was good at her job, and every doctor on O.B. wanted her to take care of their problem babies. She felt really good about this, but sometimes she knew that they never realized what pain she often suffered. She was a spinster, and these were her babies, the only ones she would ever have, and so dependent on her. To make matters worse, she hadn't felt too good lately. She just couldn't lose these babies today, at least not the Lambert child. Already they had named her, Mary Ann. She was so tiny, like a doll, with a lot of dark hair. Joan Lambert was a fragile-looking brunette. Paul was dark and handsome. With these two for parents, Mary Ann was sure to grow into a beautiful young lady. The other baby looked about the same, but so far had no name.

Suddenly Irene noticed a change in Mary Ann's breathing, and she began to work with her. Where was her replacement? She needed help, and no one was in sight. In spite of all her efforts, the tiny little soul quietly slipped away. No! No! This would never do, not the Lamberts' baby. She couldn't die! God wasn't being fair—He had chosen the wrong baby. She meant too much to her parents. Quickly, without any rational thinking, Irene removed the wristband from the tiny wrist, moved the IV bottles, and switched beds with the other infant. Now the unwanted baby was dead, but Mary Ann Lambert was alive. Irene looked cautiously around to make sure that no one had seen her and then rang for someone to help her with the dead child. No one expected her to live anyway, and to tell Leslie that her child was dead wouldn't be nearly as shattering.

From the time of the late-night call from Leslie's roommate, Mona had lived a nightmare. She had rushed to the hospital in a near panic to find Leslie being pushed to the delivery room. She ran with her, but all her reactions were automatic. She couldn't think. Bob was out of town for the night. A client had called him late in the day, and he had to stay over to conclude his business in the morning. She just kept saying over and over to Leslie, "I'm here and I love you." What more could she say to her child who was in such pain. Leslie was sleeping, so Mona slowly left the room. She was so weary and felt totally devastated.

She retraced her steps down the hall, not even sure what she had seen. She must have been mistaken. Why would Miss Morgan move the babies? The shock of the night's events had left her visibly shaken. She had to have another look at the baby. She only had a glimpse as the baby was rushed from the delivery room to the special intensive care unit for premature babies. Leslie was a blonde with blue eyes, but the look she had of the baby showed a mass of coal-black hair. Its tiny features were red and purplish from bruising, but otherwise it had looked perfect. Leslie's brother had a lot of black hair when he was born. Mona had looked around carefully as she neared the isolation unit where the babies were being cared for. She really didn't want to be seen. Oh, there was that nice Miss Morgan. She seemed such a thoughtful, caring person. She had been so understanding with Leslie. What was she doing? Why was she changing beds with the babies? That was strange. Oh well, Miss Morgan was such a good nurse—one of the best, the doctor had told her. Mona quickly left the area, thinking to come back later for another peek at the baby, her granddaughter. My God! I'm a forty-year-old grandmother, she thought.

Mona slipped quietly back into Leslie's room and sank into an easy chair. Leslie's eyes were still closed, but Mona wasn't sure if she was sleeping or still hiding from all the unanswered questions. How could Leslie have been seven months pregnant and no one know? Mona had been sewing for Leslie, fitting garments, and had seen nothing. She was certain that Leslie had not missed a single monthly period. The used pads, the tampons, and the spotting in her panties were all the visible signs. She was still the same size eight. Then another question, who was the father? Leslie hadn't been dating anyone special, mostly just friends. All totally unbelievable! How would she ever be able to explain all of this to her mother, Leslie's grandmother? She and Leslie had been so close. In fact, sometimes Mona felt that her mother loved Leslie even more than she did her. She wasn't jealous; it was simply an observation. Her parents lived elsewhere a large part of the time, so she would have to call them. How she wished Bob were here. How would he handle this? He was so proud of Leslie; she was his baby.

Thoughts kept running around in Mona's head until she thought she would surely go mad. How could she ever face her friends, the people at church, her minister? In a small town, reputation meant everything, and what about the baby? Leslie couldn't take care of herself, much less a baby. She was just getting started in college, and she had her whole life ahead of her. Certainly she and Bob couldn't start over raising a child. There was also the possibility that the baby wouldn't live. The doctor had warned her that the baby was too small and very

3

weak. She had had trouble breathing right from the start. The whirling in her head had begun to make Mona physically ill. There was so much to cope with all at once. Yesterday her life had seemed content, and today everything was in a horrible state of turmoil. She had to stop thinking or she would indeed go mad. She couldn't believe that all of this was happening. It was surely a dream, or rather a nightmare. She had to wake up—it was all too horrible.

Chapter 2

Thoughts and sounds began slowly to come into focus, and although Leslie still could not open her eyes, the happenings of the night before flashed in front of her. It was true! Last night around eleven o'clock she had given birth to a baby, a girl, she thought. She didn't know she was pregnant. Only that one time last March, and that really wasn't her fault. She had said "no," and then later she'd had her period right on time. It was too confusing.

Her eyes flickered and opened to look all around her room. She was sore, and it was difficult to move; also, she felt weak and scared. How could she ever tell all this to her mother and dad? Where was her mom anyway? She thought she was here. Here she was, a mother, and hadn't seen her baby. She'd have to think of a name and get clothes. Where would she live, and what about school? She had just gotten started in college. She couldn't stay in the dorm. What about her roommate? It was Alice who called the ambulance when she doubled over in pain, and Alice who called her mother. What was she thinking? Leslie knew her mom and dad loved her, but how could they now? She had really let them down.

Mona pushed open the door and saw the confused look in Leslie's eyes and the tears starting to trickle down her cheeks. She quickly crossed the room and cradled her sobbing daughter in her arms. Over and over she said, "I love you. Don't worry, we'll work it all out. Right now we have a beautiful little baby girl to think about. You've made me a grandmother and your dad a grandfather. We've always looked forward to grandchildren."

"Mom, I want to see my baby," Leslie said. Mona rang the bell for the nurse, hoping she could take Leslie to the nursery. She knew the baby had to be kept in the special unit for now, but she could push Leslie to the window so she could look at that sweet face.

The nurse answered the bell and said she would check to see if Leslie could be moved. She'd had a difficult delivery and had a lot of infection.

Leslie held Mona's hand and told her she had thought of a name for the baby—Angel, Angel Edwards. They held each

5

other and said over and over the name. Angel. Angel. A perfect name for their little Angel.

Mona had waited, but now she felt she had to know, so
she asked. "Leslie, who is Angel's father? He should know he
has a daughter." Leslie burst into sobs again and finally said it
was a long story, and she needed time to organize everything in
her mind. There was so much to tell. Over and over she said,
" Mom, don't hate me, please don't hate me."

Chapter 3

How happy she had been when a college boy had invited her to a St. Patrick's Day party. She was only a senior in high school, and he was the brother of one of her good friends. Granted, he was only a couple of years older than Leslie, but he was an important college man. She had begged her parents to let her go. The party would be well chaperoned, and she promised not to be late. Leslie really liked Steve. He made her feel all grown up, and she was truly excited about the party. When he came to pick her up, he brought a shamrock corsage and came in to meet Mona and Bob. They were impressed by his good manners; Leslie, by his good looks.

Leslie wore a green taffeta party dress with a fitted bodice and flared skirt. It really showed off her size-eight figure, and her matching green pumps just set her off. They were a handsome couple.

Steve complimented her all the way to the car and gallantly opened the door to help her get seated. He had borrowed his dad's car for the night, a dark blue Ford Galaxy, and had spent all afternoon under a maple tree polishing it. He liked to impress the local girls, and it really boosted his ego when they looked him over. His sister, Peggy, usually had silly girlish friends, but this Leslie was something else. He was proud of himself when he had asked her to this party and she accepted. He liked to play around a little, and at school he was considered a real ladies' man. He would only be home for a few days, so he wanted to have some fun before he went back to his studies. In fact, when he went back to school he was going to have to really study. His grades were falling down, and his parents were starting to put pressure on him. He was looking forward to a big night!

The party, held at the high school auditorium, was well under way when Leslie and Steve arrived, so they quickly joined right in. The music was loud, and everyone was dancing and laughing and having a good time. No alcohol was allowed at these parties, but it wasn't long before different ones found it necessary to step outside for a breath of air. If you didn't have a little flask in your car, someone else did. Leslie and Steve stepped outside, and one of Steve's friends motioned them over to his car for a drink. Leslie didn't drink—her folks would kill her—but Steve took a couple of hearty swigs before they went back inside. Later in the evening Leslie noticed that Steve "stepped out for air" more often. This alarmed her a little, but he seemed okay, and they were enjoying the dancing and just having fun. She felt like the "belle of the ball" with Steve. The other girls stared with envy, and Leslie felt really happy and a little dazzled by it all.

Much too soon Leslie knew she needed to be going, so she and Steve said goodbye and headed home. On the way, Steve pulled off the road onto a scenic overlook. From here you could see the lights of town, and the moon was gorgeous shining through the trees. Steve pulled Leslie into his arms and began kissing her. Leslie had never been kissed like this, and she really didn't know how to act. She'd been kissed before by her dates, but it never seemed like this. She was breathless and kind of pushed back for air, but Steve kept whispering her name and kissing her neck and lips and her throat and kept sliding her dress off her shoulders. Leslie was flattered but very uncertain exactly what to do. She didn't want to act like a dummy. He might not ask her out again, and she liked him. Finally when he lay her on the seat and started putting his hand under her skirt, she got a little nervous and scared. She said, "No, Steve, I think we should go home now." Steve didn't stop, and then it was too late. When Steve straightened his clothes and got back in the driver's seat, Leslie huddled in the corner, tears streaming down her face. The smell of booze, sweat, and semen still clogged her nostrils. How could this have happened? She was devastated! Steve was a nice boy; Peggy was her good friend. Oh, God! What had she done?

When they reached her house, Leslie jumped from the car and ran to the door. Thank goodness, nobody waited up for her. She quickly reached her room and locked the door behind her. Sometimes Mona came in to talk after a date, and Leslie didn't want her mom to see her like this. As fast as she could, she got out of her clothes and into the shower. She thought the shower would wash away everything, but no matter how much soap she used, she still felt dirty and violated.

The next morning when Leslie came down to breakfast, she was very subdued and snappish when her brother, Jake, tried to tease and question her about her new boyfriend. Jake was two years younger than Leslie and could be a pest.

The next day Steve began calling. When Mona passed Leslie the phone, she quietly said, "I don't want to talk" and hung up, but not before she heard Steve saying, "Leslie, I'm sorry—I'm sorry." Each time he called and begged to see her, she hung up. She was afraid to tell anyone. What would they think of her? She knew it was wrong, and she tried to stop him. But maybe she didn't try hard enough. Maybe it was all her fault.

Leslie was happy when Steve finally went back to school. Mona and Bob wondered why Steve didn't come back; they had liked him, too. Mona smiled to herself, remembering all the life and death matters that are a natural part of growing up. She and Bob had been honest and open with Leslie, and she seemed to have a good head on her shoulders. Leslie had never given them a moment's grief. She was a lovely young girl any family would love to claim. She was usually good tempered and always willing to help out. Her natural loveliness showed in the bouncy way she walked, with her blonde hair swinging, and her huge blue eyes sparkling. Life was full of joy just to be around her.

Chapter 4

Dr. Craig Williams slumped into the chair behind his desk and hoped to have a quiet moment alone before another emergency. The night before had really done him in. Two premature deliveries—both hard on the mothers. He could have lost them all. That Mrs. Lambert was a lucky lady. She had really worked hard for this baby, so if that little one could make it through the next few weeks she would do all right. The other poor little girl, Leslie, had no prenatal care and was full of infection and couldn't believe she was pregnant. Kids these days play around with sex without the slightest idea of the consequences. She was quite a fighter, though. That baby of hers was a little doll, and in spite of weighing just two pounds ten ounces, she seemed sturdy and strong. She must have done something right.

He would love to take a nap, and he hoped Evelyn wouldn't have any plans for this evening. He was too beat. Just then his beeper sounded, and with a sigh he responded to the call. "Dr. Williams, this is Irene. We need you at once in the neonatal intensive care unit." He rushed out of the room and almost ran down the corridor and into the isolation ward. When he saw Irene working over one of the babies, his heart sank. He hoped so much that the Lamberts would have their baby. Then he saw that it was not the Lambert baby, but the Edwards baby that was in trouble. He had really thought this one would make it, but it was too late. She was dead, and now he would have to tell Leslie. Her mother was with her, though. He didn't know who the baby's father was. Well, maybe it was for the best. Such things were in the hands of God.

With a heavy heart he walked to the desk to sign the death certificate, and then slowly he went toward Leslie's room. What he was about to do was the hardest thing doctors had to do. He hoped he could say the right things. No matter how many times he had to do this, it sure didn't get any easier.

Leslie was getting excited and a little impatient about seeing her baby. Now that she had a name, Angel, she became more real. Mona had told her she was beautiful and had dark hair, but she wanted to see for herself. She didn't know what was going to happen, but somehow it would all work out.

As Dr. Williams pushed open the door, Leslie was all smiles and bursting with questions. He walked quickly to her bedside and took her hand. His grave expression sent a cold chill through her heart. Something was wrong!

"Leslie," he said, "what I have to tell you is the hardest words a mother can hear and the saddest words a doctor can utter. Your baby passed away. She just wasn't strong enough for this world. I'm so sorry. We all did our best, you know."

The nightmare had returned, and Leslie could bear no more. She gasped one word, "Angel," and passed into oblivion. Mona also thought that the world must have ended. At that moment Bob rushed into the room and took Mona in his arms as she sobbed uncontrollably. At least now she could lean on him.

When the nurses had Leslie sedated and resting, Mona told Bob everything she knew. Plans must be made for a funeral, and what about Steve? It would have to be Leslie's decision, but they both felt that little Angel could be buried in some quiet place with just the three of them. Nothing could be gained by involving Steve at this point. He might even deny the child was his. After all, it had actually been rape.

Once more Leslie opened her eyes, and the realization of where she was and what had happened brought her mind slowly into focus. She wished she could go back to sleep and never wake up. Everything was too painful. She didn't know how long she had slept, but anything was better than having to go over and over in her head the recent events of having a baby, now a dead baby. Where were her mom and dad? She seemed to remember somewhere far off hearing her daddy's voice, but she was so very tired that she didn't want to think at all.

The first sign of movement on the bed brought Mona and Bob hurrying into the room. They had been all night in a small waiting room just outside Leslie's door. Dr. Williams wanted Leslie to have a long sleep so her body and her mind could rest and start coping with all the events of the day before. She needed time to adjust to all that had happened to her. Bob had hoped Mona would sleep a little, but throughout the night they had just clung to each other and stared teary eyed at the small form lying so still in the next room.

Leslie held out her arms, and Bob quickly rushed to hug

his beautiful daughter. He had received an urgent message at his hotel that Leslie was in the hospital, and he had returned as fast as he could. His office always knew his whereabouts and located him quite easily. Leslie was crying softly and saying over and over, "Oh, Daddy, Daddy. I'm so sorry." Bob kept stroking her hair and murmuring, "It's okay. We'll work out everything, don't worry." Mona stood helplessly at the foot of the bed and felt that her whole world was shattered. Even now she couldn't believe that all of this had happened. Somehow, it had to be a mistake. She was absolutely, totally devastated!

There were so many decisions to make, and Bob started quietly explaining to Leslie what must be done. He told her that she must decide if she wanted to include Steve in the arrangements. He spoke softly as he told her about the small lovely casket and how Angel looked like a little princess in a soft white gown Mona had chosen for her. He suggested that they have a small service in the hospital chapel with the three of them, Dr. Williams, and Miss Morgan present. The chaplain would say a few words for Angel, and they would lay the precious body to rest in the nearby cemetery. Dr. Williams thought Leslie would be able to go. There was really no reason to spread the word all over town. Anyway, they lived some thirty miles from the hospital, so it was unlikely that any of Leslie's friends knew she was even here. If some of her college friends knew she was ill, they didn't know what was wrong.

Leslie agreed with the plans her father suggested and said she definitely did not want Steve to know. Right now, she just wanted to see Angel for the first and last time.

Chapter 5

Slowly Leslie sat up in bed and tried to ready her mind and body for the ordeal ahead. Her emotions were tattered and torn, and it was as if she were outside her body just looking in. She couldn't bring anything into real focus.

Mona had brought a soft pink dress with a jacket for Leslie to wear, and she was there ready to help her dress and brush her hair. Mona loved to brush her daughter's hair; it was so soft and lovely. This was a ritual mother and daughter had followed since Leslie was a little girl. In later years it also had given them the time to talk and really feel close. Today was no exception. As she stroked over and over the shiny locks, a mass of feelings flowed between the two of them. Mona tried to absorb some of Leslie's hurt and prepare her for the next few hours. Bob would come for them when everything was ready. They hadn't had too much time to really talk, but Bob could always be counted on in any emergency.

It was a rainy dreary day. It had rained in the night, and a fine mist was still in the air. The October leaves, orange, gold, and red, were still dripping, and there was a chill in the air. Autumn was generally Leslie's favorite time of the year, not hot, not cold, and the start of the happy season of Thanksgiving and Christmas. Today was different. There was only despair. Because of the weather and Leslie's physical condition, it had been decided that Leslie and Mona would say their goodbyes in the small chapel and not go to the cemetery. Bob and the funeral home people would handle the burial.

The chapel was a small room. It contained only a few rows of seats and an altar in the front. Lighted candles were glowing. This was where everyone from the hospital came to pray and to light candles for their loved ones. It was a serene atmosphere, a restful quiet place, one in which you felt the presence of God.

Clutching tightly her mother's and father's arms, Leslie slowly entered the chapel. She saw Dr. Williams and Miss Morgan seated near the front and the chaplain standing near the tiny casket resting in front of the altar. It was white with a small spray of pink rosebuds entwined with baby's breath. It was lovely. She released her grip on her parents and slowly moved ahead where her little Angel and the chaplain waited.

15

Irene Morgan saw the look of pain and total despair on Leslie's face and thought to herself, "What have I done?" Leslie looked so different now. Maybe she did love this baby and would have been a good mother. Of course, it wouldn't be the same as with the Lamberts, but what right did she have to play God? What could she do now? She couldn't jump up and say this isn't your baby. This is the Lambert baby. Of all the years in her profession she had always done the best she could to help people. She had suffered when she lost a patient, and she had always felt good about herself. That is, until the last couple of nights when she could not get the vision of switching the babies out of her mind. Well, it was too late now, and she would just have to live with it. With a deep sigh she straightened her shoulders and her uniform as Dr. Williams reached over and patted her hand.

The chaplain took Leslie's hand and led her to the place where Angel lay. For the first time Leslie looked at the little doll face, eyes closed with long lashes lying on her cheek, and a crown of dark-brown hair. She was so tiny. Leslie touched her face and picked up a small hand. Everything was so perfect. She was indeed an angel. No other name could possibly fit. Mona had picked just the right gown, and Leslie lifted the skirt to look at the perfect legs. She wanted to hold her, just once, and so she did. She picked Angel up and pressed the little body to herself. She was cold and truly like a doll, but Leslie felt better when she again placed her in her resting place. As a child she had often put her doll babies to bed, and this was just the same. She leaned down and kissed the darling cheek, and with tears running down her face, she turned and walked to her seat beside Mona and Bob. She had said her goodbyes to Angel. She felt empty inside, not really pain, just a nothingness.

Soft music played in the background as the chaplain prayed for all of them. He offered a few words of comfort, but all Leslie could really hear was an inner voice which kept saying, "How could this have happened? I didn't plan or want a baby, but when it happened anyway, it was quickly taken from me. Is this my punishment? Am I to blame for Angel's death because I didn't want her?" These were not things she could ever say out loud, but she knew for sure that these questions would forever be in her heart and mind.

Finally it was time to go, and as Leslie stood up to leave, Dr. Williams put his arms around her. Over his shoulder she saw Miss Morgan, and she was crying, too. Everyone had been so good to her and especially Miss Morgan. How could she ever thank her for all she had done?

Mona had already taken Leslie's things from her room and put them in the car, so all they needed to do now was go directly home. Bob would handle everything else. Later, when Leslie was stronger, they would visit the cemetery. Mona hadn't had a chance to talk to Leslie, but she and Bob had decided that they would simply tell their friends that Leslie had had a severe infection following a "female disorder." No one asks too many questions about this kind of vague illness. No one need ever know about Angel.

Chapter 6

It really didn't matter that the weather was dreary outside. It was beautiful for Joan and Paul Lambert. Their own little Mary Ann was getting stronger every day, and even if she would still have to be in the hospital another few weeks, Dr. Williams had just told them he felt that their daughter was out of danger. Joan was feeling really good, too, and she was being released today. She would probably still be at the hospital just outside the special baby's room as much as was permitted, but she would also have time to get everything just right in Mary Ann's room. She had the nursery all planned before the baby was born, but there were so many little touches to do now that she was actually here. Joan had been almost afraid to do too much, just in case. What if Mary Ann hadn't lived like that other little baby? Actually, they were almost the same in size and weight and were born the same night, also.

Joan didn't know much about the other mother, only that she was young and single. It had to be terrible for the poor thing. No matter what the circumstances, Joan thought, a mother is a mother, and losing a child had to be devastating. She thanked God over and over that it wasn't her baby that died. She even felt guilty, being so happy about Mary Ann. Joan was a kind, gentle woman and very caring. She and Paul had so very much wanted a baby. They had been married for ten years, and now all their dreams of a family were finally coming true. A few years back they had had their problems. She couldn't conceive and felt that Paul blamed her, and they began to drift apart. They went to a counselor and eventually came to realize that it was only their frustrations that were causing the problems. They truly loved each other and were even thinking about adopting a child to make their family. Adopting was such a long process, so they finally decided to try some other treatments before they gave up. Fortunately it worked, and beautiful Mary Ann was the result. Paul had been so delighted when they knew for sure Joan was pregnant that he went out immediately and started buying baby furniture, a bed, a stroller, a high chair, a swing, and would have bought more if Joan hadn't stopped him.

Lovingly over the next few months they did turn a guest

room into "the baby's" room. It was always "the baby's" things, even though by then the doctor had told them it was almost sure to be a girl. They had considered names, mostly girls', but they had a boy's name ready just in case. Mary was Joan's grandmother's name, and Ann was the name of Paul's sister who had died several years before. They wanted to remember both women, and the combination "Mary Ann" seemed just right.

Paul was a professor at the state university. He was a very handsome forty-year-old with dark hair, sparkling brown eyes, and an ever-ready smile. He was extremely popular on campus, and his classes were always the first to fill up.

Joan was a dental hygienist and for several years had worked with a local dentist in his clinic. She and Paul decided while she was pregnant that she would resign from her job and be a full-time mother, at least until their baby was ready for kindergarten. At first Joan felt lost not working, but as time for the baby drew near she began to enjoy the leisure time and being pampered and pregnant. Everything about their lives seemed so good. Financially they were okay, and they had a lovely home with a fenced back yard. It was a really homey house, just the right kind for a baby.

Joan's friends had given her a baby shower, and although most everything was too large for now, Mary Ann didn't need anything more. Joan could hardly wait to get her home, to be able to bathe her and dress her and most of all to cuddle and hold her close. All she had been able to do so far was just touch her tiny hand or her little body. Sometimes she could lightly stroke her hair. When she first saw Mary Ann, she was surprised by what seemed to her a lot of really dark hair, like Paul's, but today it didn't seem as dark or as much. Babies change so fast she thought, but then she was a bit groggy when she first saw her. One thing was for sure, though: she was just as beautiful as she had remembered.

Joan had run into Miss Morgan today when she visited Mary Ann. As she came to the baby's window, she noticed Miss Morgan just looking with such a sad look. In fact, Joan thought she noticed tears in her eyes as she abruptly walked away. Miss Morgan had been so good to her the night Mary Ann was born. She really would like the chance to say goodbye and to thank her for all her kindness. Oh well, she would get the chance later since Mary Ann would be here for a while.

Paul was glad when his classes were over for the day. He had been out a couple of days, but had decided to go back today. The last few days had been really hectic. What with Joan going into early labor and the baby being so small, Paul had been through a very nervous time. It was only today he had begun to breathe easy, but all the trauma was catching up with him. He really felt tired. Tonight would be better because he would be bringing Joan home, and he hoped to bring Mary Ann home soon, too. Dr. Williams was very encouraging when he spoke with him this morning, so one day before long his household would settle down to normal. All his male friends had assured him that his house would never be normal again, at least not for eighteen years or so. The friendly teasing from the other faculty members let him know how much they cared for him. All in all, life couldn't be better. He and Joan were so lucky.

Chapter 7

Robert J. Edwards was the name on his office door, but everyone knew him as Bob. He slumped down in his chair and rocked back, closing his eyes. He had just returned from the cemetery where he had buried his grandchild. He just couldn't go home yet to Mona and Leslie. Somehow he had to get everything straight in his head, all of the unbelievable things. His daughter, who had literally been raped, didn't know she was pregnant and had had a baby who died and was now buried, and it was all over. This had all happened in the last four days. This had to be right out of a fiction novel. This couldn't be real life—not his real life. When his secretary had called him, she only knew that Leslie was taken to the hospital and that she and Mona needed him.

Bob worked for a large insurance company and had to visit some of the district offices from time to time. He had been with the company from the time he and Mona married. He had started out just as a salesman, but he worked his way up to supervisor over a number of districts.

He and Mona had loved each other almost from the time they first met. She was going to business school, and he was still job hunting. He thought she was the prettiest girl he'd ever seen, and when he finally got his friend to introduce him, he was smitten for sure. He finally got the nerve to ask her out, and from then on he knew she was the one and only for him. It was almost two years before they finally got married. By then he had settled into a new job, and everything looked rosy. Actually their lives had been really good. Leslie had been born in 1959, Jacob in 1961. A real storybook family, and now this. Were he and Mona to blame for this? Had they been too lax and lenient with Leslie? They had always been open and honest with their kids and had tried to prepare them to make reasonable decisions. Steve came from a good family. In fact, he had always had a good reputation. At this moment Bob felt he could strangle him, but unfortunately he couldn't even give him a tongue lashing. He and Mona and Leslie had agreed that Steve was to know nothing of Angel. In fact, no one outside the hospital would ever know that she had been born. Lying wasn't a part of Bob's nature, but he had finally agreed that for all concerned this had

23

to be the best way. He just didn't know what would happen next. Leslie had just started to college, and she needed to get on with her life and try to put all of this behind her. He felt certain it would not be easy for any of them to do. How should he act at home? Nothing could ever be the same. Even Jacob couldn't know the whole story, so they would have to watch what they said around him. He wasn't a dummy. He'd catch on fast that something was wrong. He suddenly felt as old as Methuselah, and he was only forty-five. He wondered if his household would ever be normal again.

Bob realized that Mona would be wondering where he was, so he called her and told her he needed to stop by the office, but was leaving shortly for home. He had to put his feelings away. He had to be strong for Mona and Leslie. They had to know he was there for them to lean on. He would do anything to ease their pain. He just didn't know how to do that. He would just have to do the very best he could, and a little time would help.

As he drove toward home, his mind wandered back to the day Leslie was born. It had been a golden day, filled with sunshine and happy anticipation. He and Mona had wanted a baby, and they just couldn't wait for her arrival. From the first moment he saw her, he felt sure the stirring of emotions in his chest was so strong that he would explode. A little bundle all pink and soft, with a little reddish-gold fuzz for hair. She had been a good baby, and in fact, even through the terrible twos she was a doll. Everywhere they went, people stopped to look and speak to her. They were so proud. Leslie had only been two when Jacob was born, and she became the little mother even then. Jacob had been a crybaby and not nearly as easy to care for as Leslie.

He smiled to himself as he remembered the ballet classes when she was six and how she loved to show off in her tutu. Leslie was always good in school—never a problem. She was popular, a cheerleader, on the debate team, editor of the school paper, and graduated second in her senior class. She was a young lady always to be proud of. Where did things go wrong?

Jacob had developed more slowly than Leslie, a little sickly when he was very young. His start in school was a little more traumatic, also. He didn't want to go. He was happy at home with his mother. Of course, that all changed when he had finally made some new friends, and he soon became a rough-and-tumble normal little boy. He had to study harder than Leslie, but he never missed the honor roll, and he was one of the star basketball players. He was sixteen now and was beginning to show more than a passing interest in girls. Bob thought he really needed to have a man-to-man talk with Jake (most of his friends called him Jake, although Bob almost always called him Jacob). He was certainly a handsome lad with nice olive skin and dark-brown hair with eyes to match. He and Leslie didn't look at all alike. Leslie had reddish-gold hair and blue eyes. She looked like Mona, but Jacob was more like Bob and his family. They had two wonderful kids. Just how did this happen? He kept asking himself over and over, but there was no answer to be found anywhere.

Chapter 8

Irene Morgan reported to the nurse's station that she wasn't feeling too well and wanted to go home early. She worked a lot with Dr. Williams, and at the moment everything seemed to be under control. The day had been especially hard for her. Just going to the chapel for the simple service for Angel had almost been too much. She couldn't refuse to go when Dr. Williams told her that he was going, and the Edwards family had asked for her to be there. Of course, he didn't know all the pent-up feelings she had or the terrible thing she had done. All through the service she kept wanting to cry out, "Your baby isn't dead," and she kept choking back the tears and trying to swallow the lump in her throat. She still couldn't believe what she had done and kept going over in her mind what her punishment would be if ever she was found out. Would she go to prison or only be put out of nursing? Just being needed and feeling useful had kept her fulfilled all these years. She had allowed her career to take the place of family, and in fact many of her patients became like family to her. Both her parents were dead, and she had only one brother and one sister. They lived away, so she didn't really know her own nieces and nephews. Once she had been engaged to be married, but that had come to a bad ending, so she had remained alone, allowing her work to become her whole life. Now she had fouled that up, too.

Yes, she needed to get home and just lie down for a while. Maybe if she could take a nap things would clear up for her. She felt a little dizzy and even a little disoriented every once in a while. She said goodbye to a floor nurse and went outside to where her old car was waiting for her. She didn't know how much longer the Toyota would run. She didn't buy it new, and she had had it for a couple of years at least. The blue paint had some scratch marks, and a few rust spots were getting more noticeable. She'd have to think about trading one of these days. She really only needed a car to get to and from work, so she had put off even thinking about it. Financially she could probably trade okay. She had always been frugal, saving everything she could for her retirement years even though they seemed forever away. Her lifestyle was simple—work and home. Occasionally she went out to a small restaurant and to a movie. She attended church when her duties permitted, but she was really a loner, allowing her work to fulfill her life.

All the way to her car, Irene felt waves of dizziness and nausea sweep over her, but as soon as she was seated she began to feel better. All she needed was to rest and maybe something to eat. She remembered that she had skipped lunch. She just couldn't even think of food while she was so preoccupied with all of the happenings of the day. Her spirits rose somewhat as she drove home. She knew that everything would work out, and she would be back to her old self in a day or so.

She climbed the stairs to her apartment and felt somewhat relieved to be home. She lived upstairs by choice. She loved to look out of her window and see the treetops swaying in the breeze, the traffic moving, and the people going in and out of the small church down the street. It also made her feel a lot safer being upstairs. You could never tell about "peeping Toms" and people breaking in through windows these days. Things were changing even in this small town. There was a certain quiet peacefulness about this place. Her living room was homey with brightly colored chintz covering her sofa and over-stuffed chair. Another recliner and a set of matching tables and lamps pretty will furnished the room. Her kitchen was small, but it was exactly what she needed. She rarely had anyone over for dinner, so the simple oval table and chairs were just right. Her bedroom was her pride and joy. She had an iron bedstead, and she kept the bed covered with a wedding-ring quilt. The bed and quilt had been her mother's, as had the cedar chest at the foot of the bed. Even though her mother had been dead for a number of years, almost too many to remember, this room was home as she remembered it as a girl. She even had her mother's rocking chair in here, and this was where she often sat and looked out upon the world.

Just getting home did make her feel so much better, and she really was hungry. She put on the kettle for tea and opened a can of chicken noodle soup. While she was waiting on this to get hot, she nibbled on some cheese and crackers. Usually she had something planned for dinner, but tonight she was just hungry and wanted something easy. When the soup was ready she carried it and a cup of tea to the living room and sank down on the sofa to eat. My, it was nice to be able to do as you pleased in your own apartment. There were no rules here. When she had scraped the last noodle from the bowl, she placed it on the coffee table, and with a sigh she stretched out on the sofa. My, this felt good. Now, away from the hospital, here in her own home, she could really think and figure out what she needed to do. She couldn't take her mind off of that Edwards girl and the poor dead baby. As much as she wanted it to go away, that terrible guilty feeling kept gnawing away at her. She had to tell someone—someone who could at least understand how she had acted so instinctively. There was only one person that fit the bill. That was Craig. She allowed herself at home to think of him as Craig instead of Dr. Williams. Ever since she had started working so closely with him some ten years ago, she had admired him and slowly come to love him. That wife of his, Evelyn, with all of her high-and-mighty ways, wasn't half good enough for him. Anyone could see that. Craig would never approve of what she had done, but he would help her. He would know what to do. With these encouraging thoughts, she drifted off to sleep, making a rippling, snoring sound that seemed to echo around the room.

Dr. Williams completed his nightly rounds and left the hospital. He needed a quiet night and lots of sleep. He had been at Maple Memorial Hospital for thirteen years. When he first came, he had planned for it to be a stepping stone to a much more sophisticated hospital, but he had been content to stay here. Evelyn had been very distressed that he hadn't moved on, and perhaps that was why he could never seem to please her. They had no children. Early in their marriage, they both agreed, with him in medical school, they simply couldn't afford a child. Then later Evelyn always had some excuse for postponing the event. Finally, it was just too late. Evelyn was fifty, and he was fifty-six. They had married while he was in medical school, and they were so in love he could hardly concentrate on his studies. Whatever happened to the feelings of those days? He had become totally engrossed in his work, and Evelyn had become a real socialite, as much as was possible here in Warren. They no longer had any common ground, so they just went on living civilly together, neither of them being fulfilled. Oh well, he had Irene and the other nurses and doctors at Maple. They were his family. He didn't know what he would do without them, especially

29

Irene. She had become his right hand. She always knew just what he was thinking, almost before he did. She was such a dedicated nurse. No one could have a better one. He pulled into the garage and went in through the kitchen. He saw a note from Evelyn, saying she wouldn't be home until late; something about a charity bizarre. He breathed a sigh of relief. It would be nice to be able to rest a little all by himself. He went up to his bedroom. They no longer shared the same bedroom, as his comings and goings disturbed Evelyn's rest. He took off his tie and shoes and fell back on the bed. My, this felt good. In minutes he was asleep.

Sometime in the night Irene moaned in her sleep and tried to turn on the sofa. She didn't wake up, but something was distressing her. The clock struck ten o'clock and she heard it, but still couldn't rouse herself. She must just be in an uncomfortable position or she wouldn't have that heavy feeling in her chest. Suddenly a sharp pain in her abdomen bolted her upright. She tried to think what she had eaten to cause such indigestion. Oh yes, it was chicken noodle soup, and there set her bowl. She hadn't even taken it to the kitchen. She got up and went to the bathroom to check her medicine cabinet for an antacid tablet. She rarely had indigestion, and this hurt pretty bad. In fact, the pain seemed to get worse. Well, if she didn't get better soon, she'd call Craig. He'd know what to do, and anyway she needed to talk to him.

She went to the bedroom, undressed, and put on her nightgown. Taking off her bra had seemed to help. Lying cramped on the sofa had probably caused this pain. She stretched out on her bed, and the pain lessened. Now if she could just go back to sleep, she'd probably be okay. She tried to lie perfectly still, then changed her position, but she was still extremely uncomfortable. Waves of nausea kept sweeping over her, and she felt sure she would throw up. She got up and went to the bathroom and brought a plastic pail to put by her bed. If she did vomit, she wasn't sure she'd make it to the bathroom. Sweat poured off her face, and even the back of her hair felt wet. She wondered if she could be having a gall bladder attack. She'd never had one, but she had patients who did, and this was the way they had seemed. She could call Craig, but it was already after eleven, and he did need his rest. She'd just tough

30

it out until morning. It probably wouldn't get any worse, so she could handle that. She did in fact finally drift off again into an unrestful sleep.

With a stabbing pain in her left arm and a heavy weight on her chest, she awoke with a start. It took her a few minutes to be fully oriented and to know something was drastically wrong. No matter how late, she had to call Craig. The nausea was back, and the pain was getting worse. She knew Craig's number, but it took her a few seconds to be able to dial. "You must answer, Craig. I need you," she kept saying to herself. The phone rang and rang and rang. At last she heard a sleepy "hello."

"Craig, this is Irene. I'm bad sick. I need you, and there is something I must tell you."

"Irene, Irene, what's wrong? Tell me," replied Dr. Williams.

"I don't know, Dr. Williams. I could be having a heart attack! Please hurry!" As she was speaking, the phone slowly slipped out of her hand, and she fell back on her bed. She could still hear his voice saying, "Irene, Irene, speak to me!"

Dr. Williams quickly dialed the hospital and dispatched an ambulance. He pulled on his pants and shirt and ran out of his room, down the hall, and out the kitchen door to his car. He didn't even hear Evelyn as she complained about his noise waking her up. He drove as fast as he dared to Irene's apartment. He knew where she lived, but he had never actually been there before. The ambulance beat him by seconds, and the paramedics were still trying to get inside. He remembered Irene saying once that she always hid a key over the door light just in case she lost hers. He felt around, and sure enough there it was. He opened the door, and the paramedics rushed in with him. He glanced around this homey living room and visually searched for the bedroom. There he say Irene lying on the bed. She was pale and in obvious distress. He checked her pulse and saw the shallow rise and fall of her chest. She was alive, but barely. She opened her eyes and saw him. "Oh, Craig, I must tell you something."

He interrupted her, saying, "Don't talk, Irene. Everything will be okay. You can tell me later."

Her mind was in a whirl, and she wanted to speak, but

she couldn't and they were preparing to take her to the hospital. Irene tried once more to say his name, but as she did, a sharp pain stabbed her in the chest, and she stopped breathing. Dr. Williams and the paramedics worked frantically to save her, but to no avail. By the time they had reached the hospital, they knew she was dead. It was 2:45 A.M. Craig was stunned! She was only forty-eight years old. He knew she hadn't felt well lately, but who would have guessed she'd have a heart attack? What was it she had wanted so desperately to tell him? He'd never know now. Grief such as he had never known before came over him, and he felt himself sobbing out the unfairness of it all, the realization that he had loved Irene, and now she was gone.

Chapter 9

Leslie stretched a little as she opened her eyes and saw that the sun was up and making a pattern across the ceiling. What time was it? Her mother must have let her sleep in. They had stayed up late last night talking and trying to make some kind of plans for her life. Physically she felt much better, but emotionally she was still in a tremendous turmoil. Here she was, back in her own room where nothing bad could ever happen to her, and she didn't want to leave it. This had always been her haven, her place of safety and of quiet solitude. She could think here. She and Mona had redecorated her room just twice that she could remember, each time making it a little more personally hers. The last time she had gotten rid of all the ruffles and the last of the stuffed animals and made it more sophisticated for an about-to-be college girl. She loved this room, and it gave her a sense of security as she lay there. She could almost imagine that none of the last few days had ever happened.

Last night, listening to her mom and dad, it had seemed rational for her just to go back to college and move on with her life. That sounded so easy. She felt she had aged at least ten years and really wanted her life to count for something. True, she had just started college and was taking basic courses. There was enough time to plan her career. Before, she really didn't know what she wanted to do, but after being in the hospital and seeing the nurses, especially Miss Morgan, she began to consider nursing as a career. It looked like a lot of hard work, but it must be rewarding as well.

Mona had called the college and got her excused for the past days. She wouldn't be dropped from her classes. She would just have to make up the work. She really needed to get back as soon as she could. Alice had called last night to see how she was doing and seemed anxious to have her back. She had felt badly about lying to Alice about what was wrong, but she knew her parents were right. There was no reason for anyone to ever know what really happened. This was Friday, and by Monday she should be back in class.

She got out of bed and stumbled around on her bedspread and clothes that were strewn all around. She wasn't too neat, and Mona was constantly trying to get her to clean her room. She sort of chuckled to herself, admitting that she was a sloppy pig. She did pick up her clothes and thought she'd surprise her mother and make her bed. She had never really understood why it was so important, although she had to admit her room looked good when she was not there living in it.

After getting her room in good shape, she went into the kitchen where Mona was baking cookies, just the kind she liked, too. Mona gave her a quick hug and asked how she felt and what she would like to eat all in one breath. They were all trying to make it so easy for her, trying to make things normal, but nothing would ever be the same again. She was no longer an innocent little girl. She had grown up, and the pain of it all would always be with her, she thought. Every once in a while, just out of the blue, she would suddenly see that little doll face, lying in her bed of satin, the closed eyes and the cold porcelain feel of her perfect hands and body. She shook her head, trying to take out all of these visions that kept popping up. She would always remember Angel, but not like this. She had to clear her brain so she could at least try to get her life back in order. She had to stop feeling sorry for herself. What had happened, happened, and she couldn't change any of that, but she could change her life and she would!

Mona encouraged Leslie to take a rest after breakfast. She didn't want her to overdo it. The doctor had agreed that Leslie should be able to return to school on Monday. She was still on medication for the infection, and she was still pretty weak.

Bob had gone to work early today, and Jacob had just left for school. He had felt a little left out with all the attention Leslie was getting. He wondered if his family would pay as much attention to him if he had to be in the hospital a few days. Leslie had always been in the limelight, and secretly he had felt a little left out. He loved his sister and would fight for her at the drop of a hat if anyone hurt her, but he couldn't help being a little jealous now and then. He had missed her at school as well as home since she had gone to college. Before, he thought it would be neat having his mom and dad all to himself, but in reality the house had seemed too quiet, and he even missed having Leslie's friends around and the battles he and Leslie had over the bathroom space. There were always curlers around and make-up and Leslie's clothes. She was messy, but he did love her even though sometimes she nearly drove him nuts. He felt real sorry for her when she came home from the hospital all pale and sad looking. It didn't look as if it had been much fun. He would try to visit with her and do something nice for her when he got home from school today.

Mona had hoped she and Leslie could have a good talk this morning. She made waffles for herself and Leslie, and they sat down to enjoy eating together. They both started to speak at once, and laughingly Mona said, "Leslie, you go first." Leslie forced back the teardrops forming in her eyes and said, "Mom, I want you to know how sorry I am. I never wanted such as this to happen, and I know the pain I've caused you and Dad. Can you ever forgive me?"

Mona reached out and took her hand and said, "Oh, Leslie, there's nothing to forgive. Life isn't always easy and we do have choices, but this wasn't your fault. We all make mistakes and misjudge people. None of us is perfect. You've always been a lovely daughter, one we've been proud of. We will all help each other get through this. We can't dwell on or change the past, but get on with the future. Time will help all our wounds heal, and although we will never forget what happened, we will put it in its proper place and be able to go on with our lives." Leslie got up from the table and went around to hug her mom. "What would I ever do without you? I know I've been a handful, but I will try to do better and make you truly proud of me. I'm so lucky to have such a wonderful loyal family."

The doorbell rang, and Mona went to answer it. It was the florist bringing a lovely bouquet for Leslie. Leslie couldn't imagine who could have sent them, and then she smiled as she read the card. "Hurry back. We miss you very much. Love, Alice, Tony, Bob, and Andrea." These were some of her college friends. They were ready for her, and she was ready for them, too; at least she would be on Monday. The future was looking brighter all the time.

Chapter 10

Jacob had ridden his motorcycle to school today. It was a Yahama 125 and the envy of some of his friends. Since he had turned sixteen his dad had let him ride to school, but he was still pretty restricted as to where he could ride. He'd wanted this for as long as he could remember, but now that he was grown up he'd really rather have a car. His dad had forbidden him to let anyone ride with him, so that meant his current girlfriend, Jessie, didn't even get a ride. He parked in the designated place and said "hi" to a number of the other students. One or two of the older students came up to ask about Leslie. Gee, there it goes again! She's not even here and she still gets attention. Anyway, he didn't know what to tell them when they ask what was wrong. He was really confused on that himself. When he had asked his mom, she had sort of whispered something about a female disorder, which meant don't ask anything more. One of those mysterious ailments girls sometimes had. He knew a few things about the birds and the bees; after all, he was sixteen. When some of the boys asked about Leslie, he just shrugged and said, "You know, one of those girl things." It got a few knowing looks, but it ended the questions. He did manage to supply the information that she would be going back to school on Monday.

Jacob was a good kid. He was quiet, and one might consider him almost shy. This could partly be credited to the fact that Leslie was always the popular front-runner. Jake had a lot of friends, especially some of the girls who thought he was a doll. He was tall, dark, and handsome, and he wasn't a showoff like some of the boys in his class. Boys liked him, too, even if he didn't clown around a lot. He wasn't a piss willy, either. He was a good basketball player, but he never tried to hog the ball and was definitely a team player. Yeah, Jake was a pretty well-rounded kid.

He kept remembering how pale Leslie had looked. When he had asked how she felt, she said okay, but the puffiness around her eyes made him think she had been crying. Leslie was a pretty good sister, even though she did get him all teed off with the bathroom mess. He had even missed that, in a way, after she went off to school. His mom and dad also had seemed a little sad when Leslie was gone. One of these days they would probably be sad or glad when he left home. Right now that seemed a long way off, and it would be if he didn't get to his English class. "Ole Stoneface," as his teacher was called behind his back, could really be tough when he wanted to, and it seemed to Jake that he wanted to most of the time, especially when it came to reading all those books and writing book reports. He never understood what all of that had to do with English. He could speak as well as anyone without all of that. The bell rang just then, and Jake hurried so that he wouldn't be tardy. He rushed into the room just in time, and as he seated himself he thought how glad he'd be when this day was over. He was going to do something nice for Leslie before she went back to school on Monday.

Bob's secretary brought him the morning paper, and he halfheartedly glanced at the sports page. He had awakened early, even though he felt like he had barely closed his eyes. He hoped he didn't have a heavy schedule today. He'd really like to go home early to see how Mona and Leslie were coping. He continued to look through the paper, and suddenly a name jumped out at him from the obituary section. Irene Morgan! She had died suddenly with a heart attack night before last. Services would be tomorrow. He couldn't believe what he was reading. She had been the nurse in the chapel with Dr. Williams. He had to tell Mona. He picked up the phone and pressed the number one. His home phone number was programmed into his office phone. He hoped Mona, not Leslie, would answer. Leslie seemed to have been very close to Miss Morgan.

Sure enough Mona answered on the third ring, and Bob asked her at once if she'd seen the paper. She said no, so he proceeded to tell her what he had read. She was stunned. This didn't seem possible. She and Leslie both liked Miss Morgan, and she had taken such good care of Leslie and baby Angel. She even cried with them at the service. She would surely be missed at the hospital. Services would be tomorrow. Somehow she would have to manage to go. That was the least she could do. Mona told Bob she would tell Leslie, and they hung up. What an unbelievable, incredible week this had been. Mona suspected Leslie would feel she needed to go to the service tomorrow, also. She had seemed to cling to Miss Morgan all through delivery, and she had taken the best of care of Angel. No one could have tried harder to save her than Miss Morgan.

Chapter 11

Joan and Paul Lambert first heard of Irene Morgan's death while they were visiting Mary Ann in the hospital. They noticed several teary-eyed, sad-looking nurses before they heard what had happened. In fact, the whole hospital seemed to have lost its momentum, and everyone walked around in a daze. Joan felt a particular loss, also. Miss Morgan had been there for her when Mary Ann was born, encouraging her and holding her hand and talking softly when the pains became almost unbearable. Later, she had taken such loving care of Mary Ann. Services would be tomorrow at 2:00 P.M. She and Paul must go. It was the least they could do. Joan also wondered where she had lived and about her family.

Mary Ann was getting stronger by the day, and she looked so beautiful lying in her small crib. Joan could just see her filling out, losing the redness, and her dark-blue eyes seemed to be watching everything around her. Her eyes were still blue, but all babies seem to have blue eyes at first. She suspected Mary Ann's would change to brown. She and Paul both had brown eyes. Although Paul was a handsome man, Joan secretly hoped Mary Ann would look a little like her. She had light-brown hair, brown eyes, and a nice olive skin. This might be their only child, and it would be so nice to have that mother-daughter look-alike. She smiled to herself and thought how ridiculous that was. Whoever Mary Ann looked like, if anyone, she would be beautiful; she already was.

Paul had spoken to Dr. Williams a little earlier, and he had told him that Mary Ann could probably go home in another few days, a week at the most, if she continued to do so well. Paul noticed how pale and preoccupied Dr. Williams looked, and of course he knew it had to be because of the death of Miss Morgan. He'd said before that she was his right hand, and now she was gone. She would surely be missed here in this hospital.

Paul joined Joan outside of the baby's room and took another good look at his daughter. He was so proud and thankful it was all over. So far he couldn't see that she looked like anyone in the family, just herself, and that was good enough for him. He could hardly wait until they could take her home where they could hold her and cuddle her and truly let her know how much she was loved. He hadn't realized how quickly such a tiny little being could fill your heart with love so strong that it was almost painful. Just thinking about it brought quick tears to his eyes. If they had lost her, he didn't think they could have stood it. God had been so good to them, and a vision of the "other baby," the one that died, flashed through his mind. He had seen them both, Mary Ann and the other one, side by side. A sudden shiver ran through his body, and goose bumps came up on his arms as he realized it could have been Mary Ann. He said a silent prayer. "Thank you, God. We will take such good care of this child you have entrusted to us." He put his arms around Joan, hugging her tightly. He was filled with such joy the likes of which he had never known before.

On Saturday it was overcast, but the weather forecast was for clearing and in the fifties for the afternoon. Maybe the weather would be nice for Miss Morgan's funeral. Mona, Bob, and Leslie drove slowly to the neighborhood church and weren't surprised to see a large number of cars. Miss Morgan had a lot of friends at the hospital, and it appeared the church would be full. The organ was playing softly in the background as they found seats about halfway down the aisle. They were just in their seats when Mona noticed another couple coming in. She had seen them before. She didn't remember where—oh yes, she did. That was the woman who had a baby the same night that Angel was born. It was their baby who was in the ICU ward with Angel. It was their baby who lived when poor darling Angel died. Ironic that they should seat themselves just in front of Leslie, Bob, and her. Their name was Lambert, she thought. Leslie probably didn't know them. She had known of another baby, but she hadn't seen the parents.

So many flowers, Mona thought. The whole front of the church was filled and down the outside aisles. Too bad Miss Morgan couldn't see all this, but then maybe she could. It would be nice if she could know what an impact she had made on so many lives. Lives she undoubtedly had made grave changes in—just working hard and giving so much of herself.

The family arrived—first, a man and some children, and then a man and woman with a young boy. Dr. Williams and presumably his wife brought up the rear. Apparently Miss Morgan didn't have a lot of family.

The minister stepped forward, read some Scripture, and then said a prayer. Dr. Williams came forward and gave a eulogy. His voice broke as he spoke of Irene and what a devoted nurse she had been. She would be sorely missed. There were tears in his eyes, and he blew his runny nose as he again took his seat beside Evelyn. She could never begin to know what Irene had meant to him through the years, and now it was too late, all gone forever.

A young woman rose and sang "How Great Thou Art," after which the minister said another prayer, and then slowly the people began to file past the open casket. Mona didn't want to see her, but there was no way she could get out without it being obvious, so she made her way along with everyone else to the front. As she passed the casket, she remembered the times she had seen Miss Morgan. In the delivery room of course, later in Leslie's room, in the special unit with the babies, and at Angel's funeral. She saw her in the halls, but the time that stood out most in her mind was while she was working with the babies.

True to the forecast, the skies had cleared somewhat and the sun was peeking through. The day had brightened, but to Dr. Williams, it was still one of the darkest days of his life.

Chapter 12

On Sunday Mona drove Leslie the eighty miles to the dormitory so she could start back to classes on Monday. Alice was pleased to see her, but somehow Leslie seemed different to her. Of course, she knew she had been sick. She had been the one who called Leslie's mom, and maybe this had been the reason she seemed so sad, and well, just changed. They hugged when she arrived, but she was much quieter and more serious somehow. Mona didn't stay long. She still had a long drive back, so she reluctantly left Leslie waving from the parking lot. They had both been a little choked up as they hugged goodbye, and Mona was blinded by tears as she finally drove out of sight. So much had happened, and she still felt that Leslie needed her, but then she would always feel this way. She had to let Leslie see that she had confidence in her and that she would always love her and have faith in her.

Leslie had dreaded going back to her room with Alice. They were the very best of friends and had always confided in each other. This time she couldn't tell her anything. Going back to school had taken on a new meaning now. It wasn't just the thing to do. It had a purpose—her life had taken on a purpose. She was now ready to prepare herself to be somebody, like that nurse, Miss Morgan. She knew she wanted to go into nursing, and she would have to work hard toward that end. She did tell Alice that she had decided to apply to the school of nursing as soon as this semester was over. Alice was a little surprised, but then Leslie had mentioned once before that she might like nursing. Alice had considered it only a passing thought. Well, who knows, she's just out of the hospital, so by tomorrow she may feel differently. She was glad to have Leslie back. They always had such fun together. Alice couldn't wait to tell Leslie about this new boy she'd met over the weekend. He was a doll and so good looking.

Leslie went to bed early to Alice's surprise. She was the one who usually had to beg Leslie to finally turn off the music and the lights so she could get some sleep. That stay in the hospital must have really done something to Leslie. She wasn't acting like herself at all. When Alice had tried to question Leslie about what went on with her in the hospital, she had

45

merely shrugged her shoulders and said it wasn't much fun being poked with needles and taking pills. Maybe a good night's rest would bring her back to her old self again.

Leslie lay for a long time just staring at a blank wall before she finally drifted off to sleep. She had turned away from Alice and pulled the covers up to hide as much of her face as possible. She didn't want to be rude to Alice, but she didn't want to talk, either. She just couldn't. Every once in a while the pain came back, out of nowhere, and she saw the little doll face and felt the coldness of her all over again.

"Will this go on forever?" she asked herself. She had truly tried to put all this behind her, had tried to forget, but how could she? If she had known she was pregnant, she might have had an abortion, or she might have told Steve. Or maybe if she had had prenatal care, the baby would not have been too small. She might have lived. A jillion "ifs" ran through Leslie's mind until she thought she would surely scream. She didn't, however, and finally from sheer exhaustion she fell into a dreamless oblivion, a nothingness that would allow her to rest both mentally and physically and to wake up more able to face the days ahead.

The days turned into weeks and weeks into months, and as Leslie healed physically, she also gained control of her emotional turmoil. She still had moments of seeing and reliving the past, but they appeared less often now, and she took on a new maturity. It was as if in the last few months she had aged considerably. Classes were more demanding it seemed, but she dug right in without complaint. She would soon be going into nursing school, and her classes now were just the stepping stones. Her friends told her it would be tough in the school of nursing, but she was clearly undaunted by this prospect. She now knew she could accomplish anything she set her mind to, and this was what she wanted.

Mona and Bob were a little surprised that Leslie had made such a quick decision. She had been totally undecided before, but they recognized the change in her, so they were eager to help in any way they could. She had seemed pleased that they were encouraging and supportive of her plans. They didn't speak often of the past. They were all hopeful that time would heal all of their wounds.

Alice still loved being Leslie's roommate; in fact, she even thought Leslie was more considerate than ever. What she didn't understand was Leslie's absolute refusal to date or even to meet new guys. School was serious business all right, but surely it wasn't wrong to have a little fun along with it. Leslie only smiled when Alice said this to her. Finally, she said, "Alice, I don't have time in my life right now for new guys and small talk. I have to keep my mind free to accomplish the goals I have set for myself. Later there will be time enough for all that." Somehow Alice knew she meant exactly what she was saying and quit trying to fix her up with someone new.

Leslie came home once in a while on weekends, and Mona drove up as often as she could to take Leslie shopping or to have lunch or dinner. Mona was beginning to feel as if she and Leslie had become good friends—mature, caring friends. It was as if two equals were discussing and deciding issues, totally unlike a parent-child relationship. This was a new experience for both of them, and certainly one that Mona was delighted to be a part of. She couldn't love Leslie more than she did at this moment.

Chapter 13

Leslie could hardly believe she was almost finished. Graduation was only a few months away, and she had made it. The going was tough a lot of times, but she just worked all the harder and somehow she got through it. It had been almost five years since she got into nursing. Where had the time gone? Now that she was about to graduate in the top five in her class she was sure more than ever that this had been the right career for her. There were times when she was exhausted from studying and bone tired from being on her feet so many hours that she felt it wasn't worth it. Then she would see that look of dependency from an old man's eyes and a pleading smile that said more than words that she was needed, and that made it all worthwhile. She loved her work, but most of all she loved to care for the babies. The tiny new helpless beings, so pink and soft, tugged at her heartstrings. The miracle of birth was still a real miracle to her, and she hoped to put her training to work in the pediatric ward. Leslie's social life had been almost nonexistent. She didn't have time for dates, and frankly she just wasn't interested in male companionship. She had a few male friends, but she wasn't ready to be involved with anyone.

Graduation day finally arrived, and Leslie was excited waiting for her mom, dad, and Jake to arrive. Jake was in college now, hoping to be a teacher and coach. He was still that "almost shy" young man he was in high school. He had lots of girlfriends, but no one in particular as yet. It had been good having Jake in the same town with her. She saw him often, and they sometimes managed to go home together. Mona often mentioned how quiet the house was now that they were both gone.

The hall was filled with parents and well-wishers, and as the graduates marched, Mona and Bob felt a surge of pride as they spied Leslie taking her seat. They knew that Leslie hoped to come back to Maple Memorial as soon as she could. This is where she wanted to work. After all, it was the events and people from Maple that had inspired her to be a nurse. She had already sent her application, of course pending her graduation.

When the speeches were finally over and the diplomas handed out, Leslie quickly made her way to Mona, Bob, and

Jake. While they were hugging and laughing and talking, Leslie spotted an old friend, Peggy Malloy. Leslie waved to her, and Peggy came right over. Her name was no longer Malloy, she told Leslie. She had been married for almost a year to a Jack Burns. Peggy motioned for her husband, and he came right over and was accompanied by Peggy's brother, Steve. Leslie gasped as Peggy said, "This is my husband, Jack, and I'm sure you remember my brother, Steve." She was startled. She hadn't seen or spoken to Steve in all these years, and there he was, as handsome as ever, smiling at her, and all she wanted to do was run. Why did he have to appear today of all days, to bring back all the haunting memories?

She still had nightmares sometimes, and memories of a tiny doll face often flashed through her mind. In fact, she was almost comfortable seeing that little face once in a while. It was etched in her memory, and she could usually conjure it up at will. Now here was Steve again. He was a big part of it, but he could never know that he was a part of anything.

Steve was very pleased to see Leslie again. She was just as beautiful, maybe even more so, than he remembered. He spoke pleasantly to Mona and Bob, but could hardly keep his eyes off Leslie. The last time he had heard her voice, she had told him never to call her again, but surely after five years she could forgive him. He was a real louse. He knew that, and he had said over and over how sorry he was. He had had too much to drink, and he had forced himself on her. Leslie was a nice girl. He didn't understand how this could have happened. He had really liked Leslie, and he blew it. He wished he had a chance to talk to Leslie alone—to tell her again how sorry he was and that he would like to make amends.

Leslie said they had to go, and she said all the right things to Peggy and Jack and then goodbye to him. Steve said he'd like to call her, but she only shrugged and said she was awfully busy. He watched her walk away, and he began to plan some way to see her again.

Leslie was sorry that Steve's showing up had put such a damper on her graduation. She could tell Mona and Bob were shaken up, but Jake thought it was wonderful seeing Steve Malloy again. He couldn't understand why Leslie had seemed so cold to him. He would never understand girls, especially his sister.

Leslie, Bob, Mona, and Jake all went out for a celebration dinner at an Italian restaurant. It was one of Mona's and Leslie's favorite places. As usual the food was great, and they were almost full of delightful breadsticks and salad before their main dishes came. They talked and laughed and never mentioned seeing Steve. With Jake present, they couldn't discuss him at all. They had all liked Steve until they knew about that fateful night. It was still hard to believe what he had done. Leslie kept remembering how handsome he was the night of the St. Patrick's Day party, and today he was the same. A little older perhaps, but he still had that same sparkle in his eyes and the ever-ready smile. Under other circumstances she would have been pleased to see him and would have gladly given him her telephone number. She didn't hate him. It was just that she still had so much pain from all that had happened, and he was truly to blame for it all. She had to put him out of her mind. She would probably not run into him again.

When Mona and Bob left that night, Mona gave Leslie a special hug and again told her how proud both she and Bob were of her. Leslie had tears in her eyes as she said goodbye. She'd be going home in a week, or maybe she'd go straight to Maple Memorial. She was sure she had been accepted there, but it would be a few days before she found a house or apartment close to the hospital.

Mona had wanted her to take at least a month off, but Leslie was really eager to get started. Warren was a modest town only thirty miles from Evanston where Bob and Mona lived. She had at first considered commuting, but she really didn't want to move back home, and she also knew that she needed to be close on the days or nights when she was "on call." She and Mona had such a beautiful relationship now, and she also felt that moving home would somehow put a strain on that. Here she was twenty-three years old, and it was time she was on her own and supporting herself. She knew her lifestyle would be slowed down a little; her mom and dad had always been overly generous with her. Not only did they pay for her schooling, but she always had all the extras, too. She might have to really budget herself at first, but she knew she could do that. Her work wouldn't allow her time for a big social life, but that wasn't what she wanted anyway. Her parents had wanted to give her a car for graduation, and she would need some transportation, but she suggested they wait until she was settled in her job and then together they would look for her a used car. In the meantime, she'd ride a bus. If she found an apartment near enough to the hospital, then she could walk. She dreaded moving. That was always such a mess. At least it would give her a chance to get rid of the stuff that somehow just accumulates.

Leslie lay down across her bed, her head filled with all the thoughts of plans that needed to be done, when the phone rang. Reluctantly she leaned over and picked it up. "Hello," she said, and then she heard his voice. "Leslie, this is Steve. Please talk to me."

"Steve," she said, "we don't have anything to talk about. Please don't call me again."

Steve said, "I just want you to know how sorry I am. Please give me another chance. I know I was a stupid fool. Give me a chance to make it up to you."

Leslie couldn't listen to anymore. She just said, "Goodbye, Steve," and slowly put the receiver back in its cradle. She didn't know how she felt anymore. Steve had been the cause of the terrible empty place inside her and of the pain that never completely went away. She had been attracted to him five years ago, and seeing him earlier had touched off those same feelings. Yes, he'd made a mistake, a big one, and she had had to pay the price. She just couldn't allow him back in her life—not now, not ever. In spite of her firm declaration, as she drifted off to sleep, she could see his smiling face, and he haunted her dreams all night long.

Leslie went to Maple Memorial for an interview and was surprised to see so little change from five years ago. There was no real question that they needed her at Maple, just mostly a matter of working out her schedule with the head nurse. She had expressed her desire to work with newborns, and she left feeling really good. She'd start to work in one week, so she would need to find an apartment and move fast. Mona came to help her and after looking at two or three, finally decided on a one-bedroom efficiency about three blocks from the hospital. The rooms were plain with simple furniture, but with a few of Leslie's things, it would soon take on her personality. She and Mona shopped for curtains and a bedspread and throw pillows to set off the bold flowered print of the sofa. A lamp and a few knickknacks made all the difference in the world. Leslie was very excited and happy that she was getting settled in her own place. Mona liked it, too, and she was so good at fixing things up. Even the fancy little waste basket and a small rug changed the bathroom. The rose-smelling potpourri added just the right fragrance. Getting her stuff moved wasn't too difficult. Even Jake gave her a hand, and by the time her things were hung in the closet and everything was put away and the boxes were disposed of, she really felt good. She was even more pleased with the kitchen, neatly arranged with a special place in front of a recessed window for a round table and chairs. She didn't think she'd cook a lot. She hadn't acquired Mona's cooking skills, but she certainly had all the necessary things when she wanted to. All in all, things were looking pretty good, and she was more than a little proud of herself. She'd graduated among the honored, got a job just where she wanted, and now she was getting settled in her own place. The only unsettling thing was that Steve kept turning up in her thoughts. She had been pretty firm the last time she spoke to him, so she didn't really expect to hear from him again. Well, that was best. She would put him out of her mind. She didn't have time for men right now anyway. The way she felt she might never want a man in her life, certainly not one who had caused her such pain and sorrow, even if he didn't know it. He knew when he forced her against her will, to have sex, exactly what he was doing. The fact she was young and totally inexperienced didn't seem to trouble him. Well, so much for Steve! She hoped she would never see him again.

Leslie loved her work! She soon fell in love with all the doctors and most all of her patients. The energy she exuded caused some of the nurses to smile, remembering in their younger years how energetic they had been. Leslie would find her own pace before she burned herself out. Leslie always took a last look at each of her patients before she finally left the hospital, never minding that she had signed out over an hour before. She lived close enough to the hospital to walk, and she enjoyed walking along breathing the fresh air and watching the people go by. She still wanted to look for a car, but she really wasn't desperate yet. She did need one, though, so she could go see her parents sometime. She really didn't know when she would have time, but a car would be nice just to take a drive or to go shopping—that sort of thing. Maybe next time Mona came up they'd take a look.

Leslie had already seen a lot of things happening in the month she had been working. Terrible accidents, kids drinking insecticide, heart attacks, strokes, and then just common illnesses that placed people in the hospital. She had come to know Dr. Williams much better, but she really liked working with a young doctor, Chris Evans. He worked in obstetrics, and she hoped eventually she would be his delivery-room nurse. She still remembered Miss Morgan and how good she had been in delivery. Dr. Evans seemed to like her well enough, so in time it could all work out. Dr. Evans had only been at Maple the past two years. He and his wife and little girl moved from a big city hospital back East. He seemed to have adapted very well to a small town, and as people got to know him, his patient load had really picked up. In fact, he was so busy that it seemed he lived at the hospital.

When Leslie first went to the hospital, Dr. Williams had stopped to talk with her. Yes, he certainly remembered five years ago, her losing her baby and all. He constantly associated Leslie's tragedy with his own in losing Irene. He had never quite gotten over Irene's death, and seeing Leslie conjured up all the old wounds again. He told Leslie how glad he was to have her here, and she assured him the past was in the past, but he saw that deep-down sadness in her eyes and knew what she felt. He felt the same way. He was little by little passing some of his patients over to other doctors and his maternity ones to Dr. Evans. It had never been the same without Irene, and the miracle of birth no longer had the magic it had once held for him. He was truly happy that Leslie was here, but he didn't want to work too much with her. It was just too painful. In a way, Leslie felt the same, but neither of them knew how the other one felt.

That weekend Mona and Bob both came to see Leslie and insisted that they go car hunting. She had a steady job, and now she could afford to have some kind of car. Jake had gotten a car when he first started to college, but Leslie had never thought too much about it. They visited several dealerships, but didn't find anything that Leslie liked or thought she could afford. Bob and Mona planned to help her money-wise, but Leslie wanted to do it all by herself if she could. They finally drove into Harry's Used Car Lot, and Leslie saw it. A Volkswagen bug, bright blue and shiny. There it sat, just waiting for her. She walked over to it, and sure enough, it was clean and sparkling inside and had very low mileage. Bob didn't think too much of a bug, but he had to admit, this one looked good as new. Now they would have to see how good the price was. The salesman came right over, and Bob did all the haggling. It was obvious to all that this was the car that Leslie had picked for herself. Strange things sometimes happen to kids. Growing up Leslie had always wanted the best and never thought of cost. Jake would have been humiliated to have been offered this car that Leslie was now drooling over. Bob and the salesman finally quit figuring, and Bob walked over to Mona and Leslie. He asked Leslie if she was sure this was the car she wanted, and she said yes. He then told Leslie that he would pay the down payment if she could pay the monthly payments. They were quite low and included insurance. Leslie was overjoyed and hugged her dad and mom right on the spot. Bob and Mona felt good. They hadn't seen Leslie this excited in quite a few years. After all the paperwork was finished, Leslie and Mona started to get in the new car to drive it home. Leslie said, "Mom, wait," and standing beside the car she solemnly said, "I christen thee, Betsy," and from that day on this Volkswagen was lovingly known as "Betsy."

As Mona and Leslie pulled up in front of her apartment, they noticed another car there and a young man getting out of it. My God, it was Steve! When he reached her side, Leslie said, "How did you find me?" Steve smiled and told her it had not been easy. On one of her happiest days here, she had to face Steve again and think back to five years ago. How could he keep doing this to her? Steve admired her car, and grudgingly she told him she had just gotten it and her name was "Betsy." Steve chuckled a little at that. He had had more than one car, but he had never named one. Steve didn't stay long, and by the time Bob arrived, he said goodbye and drove away. Leslie was glad he was gone. She didn't want to talk about him to her folks, but she was also disturbed that he hadn't stayed longer.

Maybe he was just torturing her. He simply had to leave her alone. She had to get him out of her mind forever.

While she was saying goodbye to her mom and dad and thanking them over and over again, she saw an emergency vehicle pass by, sirens screaming and red lights flashing. This was always a sign of a big problem, so she decided she'd run over to the hospital to see if she could help. On weekends the hospital wasn't as well staffed as other days. This would give her a chance to introduce "Betsy" to her other home.

Chapter 14

When Leslie entered the hospital, one of the nurses called to her and said she was needed in emergency. She ran as fast as she could, and even though she had served in emergency before and had seen a lot of bad things, this looked pretty grim. On the table was a young man, his face almost unrecognizable. A big truck had swerved to miss something on the road and had hit him head on. Dr. Chris Evans was on call, and he was certainly glad to see Leslie. He loved working with her, and she knew exactly what he needed and what he was thinking. The young man was unconscious, and he was bleeding profusely from face and head wounds. He had been in his car alone, and no one had had time to check for his identification. They had to get him fixed up first. The bleeding was beginning to subside, and Dr. Evans ordered x-rays immediately to see what kind of brain damage he might have suffered. His vital signs were pretty good, but he showed no sign of regaining consciousness. When Dr. Evans had finished stitching his wounds and stepped back for Leslie to clean him up, she was startled. This man looked like Steve. But no! It couldn't be! He'd only been gone from her house a short time. Oh please, God! Don't let it be him. As she gently cleaned his face and head, she wondered how this would change that smooth complexion and ready smile he always had.

Just then Dr. Evans returned to her side and said, "Leslie, this man's name is Steve Malloy, and he's from your hometown. Do you know him?"

She said, "Yes, his sister and I are good friends. If you'd like, I'll call his family."

She finally reached Peggy, and she tried to sound encouraging. He hadn't come to yet, but it was really too soon to know anything definite. When she hung up with Peggy, she went back to where Steve was. Here was the man who nearly destroyed her life, who had caused her pain beyond belief, and still her very being was crying out for him to be okay. Tears rolled down her cheeks, and she wondered how this person who had caused her so much hurt could put her mind in such turmoil.

Dr. Evans came in and told Leslie he was glad she had been there. He loved working with her. She had a good sensible head on her shoulders. When Leslie dared, she said to Dr. Evans, "How is he?" Dr. Evans shook his head. "I don't know. It's hard to say at this point how much neurological damage has been done. I'm hoping for the best, and that he will wake up soon. The sooner he wakes up, the better off he will be." Dr. Evans had to see another patient, but Leslie would stay right beside Steve. No one else could know what this man had meant to her, just that she knew his family. As she sat by his side, Leslie remembered back to that St. Patrick's Day party and how handsome Steve looked. That was such a long time ago, and so many things had happened after that.

As soon as Peggy hung up with Leslie, she called her parents, and now they were on their way to the hospital. Leslie hadn't told her much, but maybe it wasn't too bad. Anyway, they were glad Leslie was with him. At least she was someone he knew and liked.

Leslie met them at the door and told them that he was still unconscious, but they could, one at a time, go in and see him. Dr. Evans would talk to them as soon as he could. Steve's mom hugged Leslie and told her how glad she was that Steve's friend was with him. Leslie tried to smile reassuringly, but her heart sank when she said "Steve's friend." What had Steve told them about her? She was his date only one time in her life. Did he still refer to her as friend after what he had done? What had he told his parents about her? Leslie shook herself and tried to clear her mind of all thoughts except the care and welfare of her patient. Who he was should be of no consequence.

Leslie stayed by Steve's side, but he still didn't come to. The x-rays had shown a lot of swelling, but how much damage couldn't be determined as yet. Hours went by, Leslie always there, checking his IV and watching for any signs of change in his condition. His parents and Peggy came in at intervals and were waiting in the family waiting room. Leslie knew how hard this was on them. Steve was their only son. They just couldn't believe that this had happened so quickly to him. Neither could Leslie, for that matter. It had seemed only minutes since she saw him drive away from her apartment and now here he was unconscious. What if he never came to, or what if he was just a vegetable? He had told her before that he was sorry and wanted her forgiveness, but she just turned him away. She was taking extra good care of Steve. He just had to be okay. Dr. Evans came into the room to check Steve again, and he said, "Leslie, I'm glad you're here. I know it's your day off, and there's not much we can do but wait. He's in the hands of a higher power now. We've done all we can for him." Mr. and Mrs. Malloy and Peggy took turns sitting with Steve, and Leslie stayed close— watching for any change.

Leslie had known Norma and Jim Malloy for a number of years. Not really well, but she and Peggy had been good friends, so Leslie had visited their home often. That's where she first saw Steve and thought he was so good looking. Peggy had laughed at her when she said he was a dreamboat. Certainly he didn't impress Peggy; he was just her brother. As a matter of fact, Steve didn't seem to notice Leslie or Peggy back then, and that was why Leslie was so surprised when he asked her to the St. Patrick's Day party. She remembered how thrilled she was to be seen dancing with Steve. He was the handsomest man around and a college man, too! How quickly things changed! She didn't want to think of all the painful things now. She just wanted Steve to open his eyes and speak to her. She just wanted him to be okay, and she would tell him she forgave him and that she didn't hate him. It had been her fault, too. She could have done so many things differently if she hadn't been such a simpleton. The past was past, and it was time to put away blame. She kept saying over and over in her mind, "Please, God, let him be okay. Don't let him die."

Leslie had finally convinced the Malloys that they should get some rest, and she would call them if there was any change. No telling how long this wait would be. When Norma and Jim were settled in the family lounge, Leslie took her seat beside Steve's bed. She would stay with him no matter how long it took. He just had to be all right.

Jim and Norma kept talking about Steve and remember-ing what a happy child he had been. He was all rough-and-tum-ble boy, but he had grown up giving them virtually no problems. He and Peggy had had the usual sibling arguments, but all in all they had both given them everything they had hoped for in chil-dren. True, Steve got a little wild when he first started to col-lege. Everything was new, a wrong crowd, just the time for sewing wild oats. Thankfully he came to his senses, and after the second year, he settled down and made the dean's list. They had always been proud of Steve, and now he was fighting for his life. He was a fighter, and he just had to be all right. Norma lay her head against Jim's shoulder and tried to hide the tears that seemed to be unstoppable, careening down her face. All of this had been such a shock. "Please God, don't take our boy away from us." If she could just make him understand how much he meant to her, but he couldn't even hear her when she had talked to him earlier. Now it was wait and pray.

The night passed, and as dawn broke in the sky, Leslie tried to believe that Steve would wake up soon. She was bone tired. She had tended to all of Steve's needs in the night, and she had sat hardly taking her eyes off of him and the monitors. She knew she needed to freshen herself and maybe get a cup of coffee, but she was afraid to leave him with anyone else. She had to be there when he opened his eyes, and she knew he would. Time and again during the night, she had said his name and talked softly to him. Just maybe he could hear her. No one really knew what a comatose patient could or could not hear.

The sun was peeking through, so she adjusted the blinds and smoothed Steve's sheets. Just moving about in his room helped her to feel a little better. She stood for a minute looking down at him, and then she slumped back into her chair, the one she had occupied all through the night. As she stared at his face, tracing with her eyes every mark, she suddenly thought she saw his eyelids quiver. She shook her head and blinked her eyes to take another look, but nothing. Suddenly the eyelids fluttered again. This time she was sure, and slowly Steve opened his eyes. Before Leslie could speak or ring for the doctor, in a soft, almost inaudible voice Steve said, "Leslie?"

Leslie was holding his hand, and she said, "Yes, Steve, it's me. I've been waiting for you to wake up." He grimaced a smile and seemed to drift back off to sleep—this time, a healing sleep that he needed so badly.

Dr. Evans was elated that he had regained consciousness, and the prognosis certainly looked better. They just needed to let him sleep now. Leslie was glad to be able to tell Norma and Jim that Steve had come to and was now sleeping peacefully. They were going to remain at the hospital until he awakened and they could see him again. Steve wasn't completely out of the woods yet, but everything was now in his favor.

Some hours later when Steve really did wake up, Leslie was still there and Steve said, "Leslie, it really is you. I thought you were a dream. I thought I heard your voice speaking to me, but you were so far away that I had to come a long way to find you."

Tears of relief slid down her cheeks as she explained to Steve that she had been with him ever since the accident, and that his parents were waiting to see him. Miraculously, Steve showed no permanent brain damage and by the next day wanted to go home. Of course Dr. Evans vetoed that. Leslie was in and out of Steve's room. She had other patients, too, but Steve could hardly take his eyes off her when she was there. The scars on his face troubled him. He couldn't see some of them for the bandages, but Leslie teasingly told him not to worry. They would only make him look distinguished. She really didn't know how bad they would be, but she did know that if necessary he could have plastic surgery, and she was just thankful that he was alive and going to be his old self again soon.

Chapter 15

The smile on her face and the total look of contentment was very evident as Joan sat sipping her third cup of coffee. Paul had just left for work, taking Mary Ann with him to drop her off at school. How darling she looked, her hair pulled back in a ponytail, tied with a blue ribbon just the color of her flashing blue eyes. Many Ann loved the blue pinafore and white blouse. She had admired herself in the hall mirror before she went out. Her enthusiasm for school was unbelievable. Last year she had gone part of the day to kindergarten, but this year she was a full-fledged first grader. She never had to be called in the morning. The first sounds of the day brought Mary Ann to her feet, hurrying to get dressed, brush her teeth, and be ready to go with her papa. She always wanted to decide the night before what she was going to wear. She didn't want Papa to have to wait for her. Joan and Paul had laughed in the beginning when Mary Ann had first said "Papa." They had expected "Dada," but by the time she could say Mama, she could also say Papa. Joan had asked her one day what some of her friends called their fathers and she said mostly Daddy, but she liked Papa. That made him special, and Paul was the happiest papa in the world. When Mary Ann first started to kindergarten she had asked Joan who was going to help her while she was at school. Laughingly, Joan told her that she'd work alone on the weekdays, but she could help on the weekends. This seemed to be okay, and Mary Ann often reminded Mama to wait to bake until Saturday so she'd be there to help. She was so energetic. Joan often wondered how she could ever keep up with her.

Looking back, remembering the day she was born, being so afraid they would lose her, miraculously recovering so quickly from her premature birth, it was truly a God-sent miracle. Even the weeks and months after they brought her home, never sleeping all night, afraid something would happen to her, and not wanting to miss a single moment was precious. How their lives had changed! The never-ending joy that Mary Ann had brought to them from the very beginning was amazing. They realized that Mary Ann would be an only child, and they had seen how spoiled one could be, but Mary Ann was never like that. She was such a caring little girl, older than her years and always full of compassion for someone else. She didn't look like anyone else in the family, with her autumn-gold hair and smiling blue eyes, and she was feisty. Sometimes someone in the family teased Paul, saying, "Are you sure the iceman or the milkman wasn't blue eyed?" They were a little surprised at first, but then who cared when she was so beautiful and theirs.

Joan never knew Paul's sister, Ann. She had died in a car accident when she was only fifteen. Paul often said that his mother really grieved herself to death after that. She was driving, and although the accident wasn't her fault, she could never forgive herself for living when Ann was killed instantly. Paul's mother died with a heart attack the same year he and Joan were married. It had pleased Paul so much when she had suggested naming the baby Mary Ann, and in truth now, no other name would ever fit their beautiful child.

With a happy sigh, Joan decided she had better quit daydreaming and get busy. Three days a week she went to the dental clinic. With Mary Ann in school, she needed something to do, so she had gone back to work, but only part time. She still couldn't imagine not being at home when Mary Ann was there. She had a Mrs. Henson come in on the days she worked just to help out and to be with Mary Ann. Paul always picked Mary Ann up at school, but sometimes he had to go back on campus after taking her home. Mrs. Henson was a grandmotherly type, gray hair, a little on the full-figured side, and Mary Ann loved her almost immediately. The arrangement worked well for all of them. In fact, Joan couldn't imagine how their lives could be any better. Everything seemed perfect, and she never ceased thanking God for giving them this child who had brought such joy to their lives.

Joan went into Mary Ann's room and again smiled at Mary Ann's efforts at bed making. She didn't get the covers very smooth and the bedspread drooped a little on one side, but she always wanted her room neat. Just last year Joan and Mary Ann had remodeled her room. Most of the baby stuff was gone, and Mary Ann had helped select the new furniture. The bed and matching chest were white, and the wallpaper had tiny pink rosebuds on it. She had a bookcase which held not only her books, but an assortment of stuffed animals—her old friends— as she called them. The white eyelet priscilla curtains decorated

64

the windows and lent a feeling of homeyness to the room. Mary Ann had picked her own pink coverlet, and the white eyelet throw pillows decorated it well. It was a nice room, and Joan loved to just admire it and feel the very presence of Mary Ann. No child could ever be loved more than this child.

Joan straightened the bed and, with a happy sigh, started preparing to go to the clinic. This was her day to work, not just to daydream all day. She also wanted to do some shopping before going to the clinic. The Mayflower Shop had a big sale going. She was always looking for new things for Mary Ann.

Chapter 16

Mary Ann kissed her papa goodbye and quickly jumped out of the car to join her friends on the playground. School was such fun, and she was always eager to play with her friend, Tonya. Usually Tonya was there ahead of Mary Ann, so she looked all around trying to spot her. Sure enough, there she was running toward her smiling happily. The best times of Tonya's young years were the ones spent at school with Mary Ann. Tonya's home life was not good. She had a stepfather who didn't want her underfoot so she had to stay pretty much to herself. Her mom was okay, but she always did what he said. Rarely did she get new clothes; he didn't want the money spent on foolishness. So her mother repaired her clothes, let out the hems (You could always tell that light streak around the bottom.) and somehow managed to sneak in something new when she had to. Her mom bought things at the Salvation Army store, and that way he wouldn't know they were new. Tonya always admired Mary Ann's clothes, so fresh and so pretty. Tonya was shy at first, but Mary Ann's friendly ways soon won her over and now they were best friends. Mary Ann never seemed to notice how dowdy Tonya's clothes looked. At least they were clean. Her mom saw to that.

Mary Ann and Tonya joined hands and went skipping over to the swings and slides. They loved to swing, but they didn't play on the slide too much. Usually the boys were on the slides, and anyway it could get your clothes dirty sliding down it. They swung on the swings and talked mostly about a new puppy that Tonya thought her mom was going to get for her. She wasn't sure yet if "he" would let her have it. She hoped so. Mary Ann was excited and encouraging. She would love to have a puppy, too. The first bell rang, and the two of them ran happily to the classroom. They'd swing again at recess.

When recess was finally there the two girls made a beeline for the swings. Tonya said, "Look, Mary Ann, that slide isn't busy. Why don't we slide first?" Mary Ann was a little skittish of the slides. Sometimes she went faster than she wanted to, but she didn't want Tonya to think she was scared, so she said okay. Tonya climbed up first, and with her arms over her head she went flying down. She stood at the bottom and said,

"Come on, Mary Ann. It's like a bird flying." Mary Ann reluctantly climbed the ladder and seated herself on the slide. She really didn't want to let go, but she knew she had to. With a deep breath she let herself start down the slide. She was going too fast, so she put her arms down and grabbed the sides to slow herself down. Just as she did so, she felt a sharp burning pain in her arm, and she felt splatters hitting her in the face. Tonya screamed as Mary Ann fell at the bottom of the slide. Blood was spurting from her arm and all over her dress and shoes, and Tonya was trying to help her up. Mary Ann felt dizzy and a little sick, and Tonya yelled for the playground teacher. The principal came running, also, picked Mary Ann up, and told the teacher to call her parents, he was taking her to the hospital. They had tried to wrap her arm in a towel, but blood was still running off the tip of her fingers and her arm hurt. She tried not to cry, but she was feeling so sick. The principal kept talking to her, telling her that everything would be okay and that her mom would be there soon. As they pulled into the emergency entrance they were met with a gurney. Mary Ann was placed on it and rushed into the emergency room.

The secretary at school called Mary Ann's house and the housekeeper, Mrs. Henson, answered. No, Mrs. Lambert wasn't there. She had already left for the clinic. She called the clinic, but Mrs. Lambert hadn't arrived yet. She then tried Professor Lambert at the college, but he was off campus during this hour. She left messages at all three places, but didn't know what else to do. She would just keep calling. She didn't know how bad Mary Ann's arm was, but the teacher had said it was ripped open.

Dr. Evans was trying to stop the bleeding. This child had lost a lot of blood. Her arm was badly torn, and the main artery was severed. He knew the pain was terrible for her, and she kept asking for her mama and papa. She would most likely need a blood transfusion, and he wished strongly for her parents, also. He was having her blood typed, and the nurse came in to tell him Mary Ann was AB negative. That was pretty rare, and they didn't have that type in storage. He remembered that one of the nurses in the hospital had that type. Once before in an emergency she had given blood. They made a quick check, and sure enough Leslie Edwards had that type.

The loudspeaker called her name, and Leslie went immediately to answer the call. Of course she'd give blood. She went as fast as she could to the lab where they were waiting for her. All the technician knew was that some child had gotten hurt at school, and Dr. Evans wanted the blood ready in case he had to use it. Leslie shrugged and laughed. "At least I get a glass of orange juice." She always gave blood for the Red Cross, and once before had given blood in an emergency at the hospital.

Mona was at the hospital this morning. She did volunteer work twice a week. She loved being near Leslie, and she had a real feeling of compassion for some of the patients. She read to them or wrote letters or just generally tried to cheer them up. She loved the children's ward best, and that's where she was when she heard Leslie's name called. Of course that wasn't unusual. Leslie was always needed somewhere. She didn't know how Leslie could do so much.

As soon as Joan walked into the clinic the receptionist told her that the school secretary had called, that Mary Ann had been hurt, and that she was to go immediately to the hospital. Joan felt a sick gnawing in the pit of her stomach and asked the receptionist to call Paul as she hastily went out the door. She automatically drove toward the hospital, not being conscious of any of her surroundings. She just knew she had to get to Mary Ann. She couldn't even imagine what had happened.

Paul had returned to his office and was just about to go to his classroom when he got Joan's urgent message. He asked another teacher to see to his class as he ran out to his car. No use to panic, he didn't even know what the problem was. He did know that he had to get to the hospital as fast as he could for Mary Ann and for Joan.

Dr. Evans shook his head as he worked on Mary Ann's arm. He had the bleeding stopped, but when he had a good look at the ragged, torn arm, he felt sad. At best this would leave a hideous scar. Of course, later, plastic surgery could help, but right now he had to repair it as best he could. He had given Mary Ann enough medicine that she was feeling no pain, but she was conscious and still asking for her parents. He didn't like the ghostly look of her. She needed a blood transfusion. He had the blood ready, but he needed her parents permission to give it.

Paul and Joan arrived simultaneously, and both jumped from their respective cars and ran into the hospital. A nurse quickly guided them just outside of the emergency room. Dr. Evans met them and briefly told them that Mary Ann had cut her arm on a piece of metal sticking up from the slide. He assured them she would be okay, but he needed their permission to give her a blood transfusion. He had the blood. They both agreed immediately, and he asked them to wait a few minutes and then they could see Mary Ann.

Paul put his arms around Joan, and they just held each other. Dr. Evans had said she'd be okay, but what wasn't he telling them? They either one would have gladly given blood for Mary Ann. Paul was type O, but Joan didn't know her type. It was good the hospital had blood. It saved time.

In a short while, although it seemed like forever, a nurse came and told them they could see Mary Ann. Joan felt faint when she saw the little pale face and the arm bandaged from elbow to wrist. They had cleaned her up, and she had on a hospital gown. Mary Ann sleepily opened her eyes and said, "Oh, Mama, Papa, I ruined my dress. I got blood all over it and my shoes and socks, too." Joan patted her hand and said, "Don't worry about that. I'll take care of it." Dr. Evans told them what a brave girl she had been, and that he wanted to put her in a room and keep her for a couple of days. She had been through a lot. He would talk to them later in his office when Mary Ann was settled and resting. That was what she needed now. Mary Ann kept trying to talk all the way to her room. "Mama, I got blood on my hair and my arm really hurt. I only cried a little, and Tonya was playing with me, but she didn't get hurt and she called the teacher." Tears welled up in Joan's eyes, and she just kept patting her hand and telling her how proud she and Papa were of her and how much they loved her. As soon as she was in her room, the nurse gave her something to make her sleep, and with a smile on her face she drifted off peacefully.

Dr. Evans explained to them that her arm would function fine, but it would probably be badly scarred. In time, he said, they might want to do plastic surgery, but for now she just needed to heal. He also told them one of the nurses gave blood for her.

Chapter 17

Mona was doing her volunteer work again today. This time she was going to read fairy tales to some of the children. She always liked this part, but she also felt so sorry for some of the little ones. Some would never go home. She hadn't seen Leslie since she was here two days ago. Maybe they could have lunch today.

As she was passing one of the rooms in the children's wing, she backed up to look in and nearly fainted. There sitting up in bed, obviously getting ready to go home, was—"Oh my God"—Leslie. The same hair and bright eyes. The same smiling face. She remembered Leslie so well at that age, and this child was the spitting image of Leslie. She tried to control her emotions and stepped into the room to say hello. The little girl smiled and said, "Hi."

Mona asked, "What is your name, honey?"

She said, "I'm Mary Ann Lambert, and I'm waiting for my mama. She's checking me out, and we're going home. I hurt my arm at school, and I had to have some new blood." Lambert? Where had she heard that name? Oh yes, that was the people's name who had a baby the same day that Angel was born.

Suddenly there flashed back in her memory, Miss Morgan, and looking through the glass and seeing Miss Morgan move the IV bottles and then change places with the beds. Was she losing her mind? This child said she had to have new blood, and just two days ago Leslie gave blood for some child because her type was rare and the same as Leslie's. My God, could this possibly be true? Could Miss Morgan have changed places with the babies, and could the Lambert baby have died and before her now sat Angel? Mona's knees began to shake, and she knew she had to get out of there. She said goodbye and went quickly to the restroom to wash her face and try to regain her composure. Surely she was wrong, but this child was Leslie all over again. Even her voice. Mona tried to remember the Lamberts. They both had dark-brown hair and eyes. After some time, Mona believed she had herself under control and went back to the room to see the child again. To her dismay, she was gone. Surely her eyes hadn't played tricks on her. She would have to find out where the Lamberts lived. She couldn't tell anyone. She would just have to try to see the child—Mary Ann—again. Mona truly believed she had seen Angel. Leslie's Angel.

Maybe she could talk to Dr. Williams. He might have some explanation. She was in such an emotional state she didn't know if she could read to the children, but they were expecting her. She tried to pull herself together, left word at the nurses' station for Leslie, and went to the children's ward. Their happy faces when they saw her temporarily relieved her mind of all the questions. They even made her start to wonder if she had imagined everything.

Mona met Leslie for lunch, and as they sat in the cafeteria, she asked Leslie who she had given blood for. Leslie said it was for some six-year-old girl who had gotten hurt at school. "Did you see her?" Mona asked.

"I didn't get a chance," Leslie said. "I meant to stop by her room, but I got real busy, and by the time I got there she had already gone. Dr. Evans was very impressed by her. He said she was a doll with beautiful blue eyes. Sort of like mine, he said."

Leslie had wanted this opportunity to tell her mother that she might be going out with Steve. She didn't know how Mona would react. In fact, Leslie wasn't sure how it would be for her. After Steve had left the hospital, he had called Leslie several times just to talk—just nice and friendly talk. How he appreciated her taking care of him in the hospital, and how he wanted to make up for everything. He didn't know that there was no way anyone could make up for what she'd lost. But then he'd never know that. Finally Steve had asked her to go to dinner and a movie, and she had said yes. When she told Mona, she was surprised at how quiet her mom was. She simply said, "Leslie, I don't want you to get hurt all over again. Maybe you can forgive Steve, but it may take me a while longer." Leslie asked Mona to talk to her dad. She didn't want to do anything behind their backs, and, no, she wasn't sure about this, but she did like Steve. It always gave her a thrill to see him. She couldn't hate him. The past was past.

Leslie noticed that Mona was preoccupied all during lunch, and when Leslie mentioned it she simply said she had been both happy and sad as she read to the little ones that morning. Leslie could understand this. She was often affected this

72

way by the children. Some you could help, some you couldn't and those were the heartbreakers. Such was life at the hospital.

A look at her watch told Leslie she had to go back on duty, but Mona stayed on to finish her coffee. It was almost cold, but her mind was a long way away so she didn't even notice. She couldn't get the picture of that little girl out of her mind. Something was wrong here. She finally decided she would go and talk to Dr. Williams. How else could she be sure if he knew something about this strange situation? She paid her check and went back to the hospital floor that contained most of the doctors' offices.

Of course Dr. Williams's receptionist wanted to know if she had an appointment. When Mona said no, the receptionist just shook her head and said, "He's full up today."

Mona told her, "I'm not sick. I simply need a few minutes to talk to Dr. Williams. It's most important."

"Well," she said, "it's not quite time for his next patient and the doctor is already back from lunch, so let me see if he can see you now."

In just a minute, Mona was directed into Dr. Williams's office. He wasn't sure he remembered her at first, but she reminded him of Leslie and how they lost Angel. Yes, he remembered the service in the chapel. That was the night Irene died. He'd never forget that. "How can I help you, Mrs. Edwards?" he asked.

Mona didn't really know where to begin. As last she said, "Dr. Williams, I know this will sound crazy, but I just saw another child, Mary Ann Lambert. She was the baby born the night that Angel was. She's now six years old, and she looks exactly like Leslie, Angel's mother. Also, she had to have a blood transfusion, a rare type, AB negative, and Leslie gave it for her. They matched. I also saw something six years ago that I wondered about, but it didn't seem significant until now. On the day that Angel died, I was looking through the window at the two babies, and I saw Miss Morgan take off the armbands, move the IVs, and change places with the cribs that held the babies. Could it be possible that Angel wasn't the dead baby, that in fact it was the Lamberts' baby that died?"

Dr. Williams had a pained expression, and he said, "Mrs. Edwards, you are letting your imagination run away.

73

Whatever you saw Irene doing, it was part of her duty. She was a most dedicated nurse. That's why we used her in the baby unit. What you are suggesting is next to impossible. As for the blood transfusion, I'm sure it was just coincidence that Leslie's blood matched. I dare say, Mrs. Edwards, you will see many children that will remind you of something your own child did at that age or will have the same look. I'm glad you came to talk to me about it. Perhaps it will help you to clear your mind. I'm sure your loss of Angel is and always will be a tragic one. It was also to Irene and to me."

Mona knew she was being dismissed, so she thanked Dr. Williams and left his office. He was probably right. She had just gotten carried away when the little girl looked so much like Leslie. Yes, he was right. She had years ago seen children that reminded her of Leslie at the same age. Blood type—pure coincidence and the child's parents weren't there in time to give blood. She tried to breathe a sigh of relief. She would certainly not tell anyone how foolish she had been. She went by to visit a couple more patients before she decided to go home. She didn't know how she was going to prepare Bob for the fact that Leslie was beginning to get involved with Steve Malloy again. It took a lot of restraint to keep Bob from finding Steve and "making him pay," as he had put it. He had only calmed down after he realized that Leslie would only be hurt more if he had confronted him. Even after six years, Bob still felt bitter. He hadn't gotten over the fact that his little girl had been hurt, and he couldn't do anything about it. He had agreed with Leslie and Mona. They must forever keep the secret of Angel.

After Mona left his office, Dr. Williams sat staring into space. He couldn't believe what she had told him, and he had answered her in the only logical way. Irene was the best baby nurse anywhere, but what was it she so desperately wanted to tell him just before she died? He had shushed her up, but the look on her face and pleading eyes kept wanting to tell him something. Why would she have moved the babies if what Mrs. Edwards said was correct? Irene had so wanted the Lambert baby to be all right. She had expressed her concern for the family. My God, such a thing couldn't have happened in this hospital. He simply had to get this out of his mind. The very thought was preposterous.

Chapter 18

Joan checked Mary Ann out of the hospital and, after last-minute instructions from Dr. Evans, walked beside her as a nurse pushed her in a wheelchair. Mary Ann thought that was pretty neat, but she said, "Mama, we don't have a wheelchair at home." Joan laughed and said, Mary Ann, your arm was hurt, not your legs." She hadn't had a look at Mary Ann's arm. The doctor told her it was pretty bad, but in time, after the stitches were out, it would start looking better. When Mary Ann was older and if the scars bothered her, they could be repaired. For now she just needed to concentrate on the arm healing. Joan would take her back in a week. She still felt chills every time she thought about how scared she was going to the hospital and seeing the little pile of bloody clothes and shoes. Mary Ann had been concerned about her pinafore. She was always careful with her clothes, and she had kept saying, "Mama, blood got on everything, even the principal's shirt when he carried me."

Paul and Joan had gone to the school to check out the slide where Mary Ann got hurt. Sure enough, one side had a strip of torn metal sticking up. It was a miracle some other child hadn't been hurt on it before. Of course, that slide was removed from the playground. Joan had also wanted to thank the teachers and principal for their quick action in getting Mary Ann to the hospital. This most likely saved her life. It certainly made Paul and Joan appreciate more the people in whose care Mary Ann was every day at school.

While Joan was at the school she had a chance to talk to Tonya. She'd seen her before when she picked up Mary Ann and knew she was a good friend of Mary Ann's. Tonya shyly sidled up to her and asked if Mary Ann was okay. Joan explained to Tonya all that had happened and that Mary Ann would be back at school in a day or two. Tonya smiled and said she had missed her and that she had been scared when she saw all the blood and the principal taking her to the hospital.

Joan couldn't help but notice the faded, let-out dress Tonya was wearing. Her hair was shiny clean and pulled neatly back in a ponytail, but there was something about this child that made her feel sad. Maybe she could meet her mother and get to know Tonya better. She was the only friend that Mary Ann really talked about all the time. She and Paul had been so wrapped up in Mary Ann that they hadn't even thought that other children might not have it so good.

Joan asked Tonya if she would like to come and visit Mary Ann. She said, okay, yes, but she had to go straight home after school. Joan asked for her phone number and said she'd call her mother. Tonya hesitated, but then gave her the number. She really would like to see Mary Ann, but she didn't think "he" would let her go. His name was Ralph, but Tonya always thought of him as "he." Ever since he had married her mother almost three years ago, things had been different around their house. Her mother never got to spend time with her if he was there. She had to be all the time waiting on him. He wanted Tonya to be in her room and not making any noise. Even when he came to say good night, Tonya didn't like it. He always put his hands on her and sort of rubbed around on her body. His hands felt rough and scratchy, and his breath always smelled bad. Her mom didn't have to work anymore. Ralph paid for everything. He just didn't want to waste money on stupid things for Tonya.

Joan called Hannah Emerson and explained all about Mary Ann and how she would like for Tonya to come over after school and stay for supper. She would bring her home early. It would really help Mary Ann if she could. The traumatic experience had left her a little depressed. Hannah hesitated. She didn't know the Lamberts, although every time she and Tonya were alone, Tonya couldn't stop talking about her friend, Mary Ann. Finally Hannah said, "We don't live far from school, and sometimes I walk over just to walk back with Tonya. Why don't I meet you there after school and then decide, if Tonya wants to go." Joan quickly agreed, smiling to herself. Mrs. Emerson was being very cautious of Tonya and well she should be. She'd be there after school, and it would certainly be a surprise for Mary Ann if she could bring Tonya to see her.

After Hannah hung up, she started having misgivings about meeting Joan Lambert. She just knew Ralph wouldn't like it, and he did have a temper. He never let Tonya do anything. No wonder she was so happy to go to school. This time he'd just have to be mad. Joan had sounded so nice on the phone, and Tonya was always talking about Mary Ann. It was time Tonya had a little fun, even though she knew they would both pay for it in some way. Ralph was a good provider for everything except for Tonya. She had thought when she married him that he loved her baby, too. Tonya was a little over three then, but it didn't take long to notice how he kept looking at Tonya and pushing her away from him. Tonya's father had died of leukemia when she was hardly a year old. Tonya didn't remember him, and Hannah had thought Ralph would be a good father for Tonya. It really hadn't turned out that way, and Hannah was often disturbed by it. In fact, she really didn't know how to handle the situation. It seemed as if she only made matters worse if she mentioned Tonya to Ralph. Getting out of the house to visit a sick friend would be great for Tonya. If Mrs. Lambert was as nice as she sounded, Hannah was going to let Tonya go, no matter what Ralph said or did.

When Joan arrived at the school, Mary Ann had come with her. As soon as Tonya saw Mary Ann, she came running, and the little girls hugged and giggled, both talking at once. Hannah was there waiting, and as soon as she saw Joan and Mary Ann, she was pleased to let Tonya go. Joan insisted on giving Hannah a ride home, then she would know where they lived when she brought Tonya back. The two girls were in the back talking like crazy, hardly aware that Hannah was getting out at home. Joan said goodbye, and Hannah waved as they drove away. She'd try to fix Ralph's favorites for supper, and maybe that would put him in a good mood. You could never tell how Ralph was going to be. He was moody and changeable.

Mary Ann and Tonya held hands as they went up the walk to the house. Mary Ann's hurt arm was in a sling, and Tonya was careful not to bump it. She was impressed by Mary Ann's house, but when they went into her room, Tonya's eyes really bugged out. The room was so beautiful, just like a storybook. Oh, she had a room of her own, but it was so plain, and her furniture was old and scarred and the walls were dark with only a shade on her one window. Her mother kept it neat and clean and would probably paint and fix it up except "he" wouldn't let her. Sometimes she wished he would go away and they would never have to see him again. She didn't like Ralph one bit, but mostly he scared her, and sometimes she heard her mother crying and Ralph yelling.

77

Mary Ann and Tonya talked and played, and when Paul came home, Mary Ann hurried into the living room to meet her papa. Paul hugged Mary Ann and solemnly shook Tonya's hand. "I'm so glad to meet you, Tonya. Mary Ann talks about you all the time. Thank you for coming to help us cheer up Mary Ann. You are just what we needed," he said as he patted her head. Tonya beamed and wondered why Ralph couldn't be like Mary Ann's papa. She hoped that she would get to come back here again.

Hannah was a little nervous as she prepared chicken with rice, one of Ralph's favorites, and a chocolate pie. She really didn't know how Ralph would react to Tonya being gone. He was such a stickler about her coming straight home from school. Maybe she was wrong, and he would be happy that Tonya had such a good friend.

When she heard Ralph drive up, she met him at the door with a welcome hug and a smile. "What brought this on?" he asked. "And what are those delicious smells?"

Hannah breathed deeply and said, "Oh, I made some of your favorites tonight. I knew you would enjoy a good meal."

"Well, you are right about that," he said. "I had a lousy day today. Nothing seemed to go right." He looked at the table and saw only two plates and laughingly said, "Aren't you eating?"

Hannah knew the time had come, so she tried to sound cheerful as she said, "Oh yes, I'm eating. Tonya went home with a friend. I thought how nice it would be for just the two of us tonight." Ralph began to ask all sorts of questions. "Where did she go? Do you know these people? When is she coming home?" Hannah tried to explain that Mary Ann was Tonya's best friend at school, and that she had met Mrs. Lambert and that she would be bringing Tonya back soon after supper. "Mary Ann was the little girl who got hurt at school," Hannah continued.

Ralph took her by the shoulders and turned her to face him. "You know you should have asked me before you let her go. You never know what kind of people are out there." He shoved her away from him, and she caught herself on the cabinet to keep from falling. "This was a stupid thing for you to do," Ralph continued. "First thing I know you'll be inviting some little brat over here."

78

Hannah started putting the food on the table as Ralph slumped down in his chair. The food looked and smelled really good, but her appetite was all gone. She knew she had to eat with him, so she sat down, and after serving Ralph's plate, she put as little as she dared on her own plate. Of course, Ralph noticed and said, "What's wrong with this food that you took so little? Have you been snacking all afternoon so you aren't very hungry?" Hannah shook her head and continued to try to eat. She could hardly swallow, and she felt tears welling up in her eyes, but she couldn't let Ralph see that. It would only make him madder. She swallowed hard and tried to make pleasant conversation, asking Ralph how he liked the chicken. He only grunted an answer, but she breathed a sigh of relief. He was beginning to calm down so maybe the worst was over. By the time she served him chocolate pie, he was in a much more pleasant mood and seemed to have forgotten Tonya altogether. She could only hope that he wouldn't make a scene when Mrs. Lambert brought Tonya home. Hannah didn't understand Ralph's attitude about Tonya. He never wanted Hannah to buy anything except the bare necessities for Tonya. She loved Ralph; at least, she had truly believed they were in love when they married. She just didn't seem to be able to figure out what had happened to him. He could be kind and gentle, but these were qualities that she had begun to see less and less as time went by. He made Tonya spend so much time in her room, but then every night he went to kiss her good night. He was a caring man; he just had a different way of showing how much he loved her and Tonya.

Chapter 19

Leslie couldn't get her hair to do what she wanted it to. Perhaps it was because she was a little nervous and still not sure if she had done the right thing in accepting a date with Steve. Leslie started checking her wardrobe for what to wear hours before Steve would be there, and she still wasn't sure. She didn't know why she felt so flustered. It was only dinner and a movie, and they had talked several times on the telephone, but she hadn't seen him face to face since he left the hospital. He had told her the scars were pretty bad at first, but were getting less and less noticeable.

She finally decided on a simple blue shirt-waist dress with pearl buttons. She'd wear her pearl earrings and black patent shoes. The dress really brought out the blue of her eyes, and she admitted to herself that her eyes were one of her best points. She finally got her hair under control, and as she looked herself over in the mirror she was pleased. She wanted Steve to be pleased, also, although she didn't really understand why it mattered so much what he thought. This was simply a friendly date. Maybe the only one. They might never even want to go out again. While Steve was in the hospital, Leslie had seen what she believed was a great change in him from six years ago. He was still a boy back then, and now he had grown up. She certainly had to admit he was in her thoughts more and more, and not because of the bad times, either. Leslie had dated a few fellows in the past years, but no one made her feel that it was even worthwhile. She just wasn't interested. She had her school work to do and later her job, and so far that was all she needed—until now. She hadn't been this excited since she was a kid at Christmastime, and it was only over a date.

Steve had taken longer to get ready than usual, making sure he didn't miss a whisker and pressing his hair down in all the right places. He had finally put on a pair of brown slacks with a tan polo shirt and brown shoes and socks. He didn't want to overdress, but he didn't want to just wear jeans, either. He had thought all week about this date, ever since Leslie had agreed to go. He hadn't quite gotten over the events of their last date six years ago and was still ashamed of the way he had behaved. He couldn't imagine how he could have done such a

81

thing, forcing himself on her, and he wouldn't blame her if she never spoke to him again. He tried to find excuses for himself. He had been young and stupid, and he had been drinking, but none of the reasons could justify what he had done. Leslie had been a young girl who trusted him. He had failed her miserably. He rubbed the long scar along his cheek and decided he looked his best, and it was time to go. He hadn't been this nervous ever before on a date.

Leslie heard a car stop and looked out of her window and saw Steve getting out of a new red Ford. She knew he'd gotten a new car after his accident, but she hadn't seen it. She smoothed her dress and with a deep breath went to open the door for Steve. They looked at each other, and both started to speak at the same time.

"You first," said Steve laughingly.

"I was just going to say how well you looked and that most of your scars are gone," Leslie said.

"Yes, I'm lucky. You taking such good care of me in the hospital really helped, but what I was going to say was that you look beautiful."

Leslie smiled and pulled the door shut behind her as they walked out to the car, and Steve opened the door for her. She said, "This car really makes my 'Betsy' look bad. It's beautiful and has that new car smell." Steve said he hadn't really meant to get a new car anytime soon, but his car had been totaled in the accident and this seemed the sensible thing to do.

They drove to the local steak house. There weren't too many choices in Warren, but Steve and Leslie had discussed it on the phone and this is where they had decided to go. Both of them liked steak, and this seemed the likely place. Leslie had wondered what they would talk about, but it didn't seem to be a problem. After they had ordered, she a small filet mignon, and he a T-bone, Steve told her all about Peggy, how happy she was and that she was pregnant. They were hoping for a boy, but were already picking out names for either sex.

Leslie hadn't meant to talk about her brother's problems, Jake's, but she ended up telling Steve how one night last week, the police had called her mom and dad. Jake had been arrested for fighting, and he had been drinking. It seemed that some man had made derogatory remarks about "that sexy nurse" who turned out to be Leslie, and Jake had powed him one, then the fight was on. Jake ended up getting the worst of it, a black eye and a split lip. Bob and Mona could not believe Jacob had behaved in this manner, but they soon knew it was true when they saw him in jail. Not only was he bruised up, but he smelled like a brewery. The sheriff let them take him home, but he had to appear the next afternoon to face charges of disorderly conduct while under the influence. Bob and Mona were both shocked and hurt at Jacob's behavior. They were not a drinking family. They never served alcohol, and Bob couldn't remember the last time he had had so much as a glass of beer. Whatever could have gotten into Jacob to act this way? They took him home and cleaned him up, and he fell into bed to sleep it off. Jacob had never caused them any trouble and now this. He was doing okay in school, although Bob and Mona both thought he could do better.

When Jake woke up in his old bed at home the next morning, he knew he was in for it. He didn't exactly know what happened. He did remember this big guy talking about Leslie, something about how sexy she was. He just kept on and on, and then Jake hit him. He didn't remember much after that. He didn't know what made him do such a stupid thing. He had had several drinks, but he thought he was okay. He sometimes had a beer, but he really wasn't a drinker. He didn't know how he could explain this to his mom and dad. He couldn't even explain it to himself. On top of everything else his mouth tasted like cotton, and he had a splitting headache. His mouth was swollen and sore, and a look in the mirror showed him a greenish-blue eye and cheekbone. He rinsed his mouth out and dabbed at his face. He took a shower and tried to comb his hair. He felt lousy. If this was what "drunk" was all about, he wasn't interested in any more of it.

When Leslie finished telling Steve, he just said, "You know, Leslie, sometimes a person does a stupid thing. There's really no answer as to why. Jake's a good person; he just made a mistake. Thankfully, no one was hurt, but you can almost certainly be sure he won't get into that kind of problem again." She felt better after Steve's remarks, and she hoped he was right. She and Jake had been very close growing up, and except for a few sibling rivalries, they had had a lot of fun together.

When their food arrived, they both ate heartily. Leslie had been afraid she wouldn't be able to eat, but things had gone so well and seemed so comfortable with Steve, and then her steak was nice and juicy, just the way she liked it. They had plenty of time before the movie, so they lingered over coffee and just kept talking about everything. Finally, it was time to go. Leslie almost hated to leave. Sitting there with Steve had seemed the most natural thing in the world. He had filled her in on the last few years—about himself and people they both had known growing up. It made Leslie feel all warm and happy. Of course, in the movie they ate popcorn, although they both declared they were so full they didn't know where they'd put it, and during the scary parts, Steve held her hand.

When the movie was over and they were back in the car, Leslie said, "Steve, I've had a marvelous evening. Thank you so much." It was still reasonably early, but Steve knew Leslie had to go early in the morning to the hospital, so he didn't even suggest they ride around. Anyway, Leslie might be thinking it was like the last time they had gone for a ride. He didn't want to make a wrong move now. He really liked Leslie. In fact, he had had her on his mind a lot in the last few years. He'd dated quite a lot, but no one measured up to Leslie.

When they reached Leslie's house, Steve opened her door and walked up the steps with her. He wanted to kiss her, but he didn't know how she would react. He'd just have to take it slow and easy. Again Leslie told him what a great time she'd had, and Steve said, "Leslie, can we see each other again soon? I really love being with you."

Leslie hesitated, but only briefly, before she said, "Why, yes, I'd like that." As she went inside Steve just touched her shoulder lightly and said good night. Leslie wondered why he didn't kiss her, but she wasn't sure how she would have reacted, so it was just as well. Maybe next time. She kept smiling as she dressed for bed and really didn't know whenever she had felt so happy and contented. She kept seeing Steve's smile and the sparkle in his eyes and the scar that was still prominent on his face. It just made him look more interesting.

Leslie turned over and over in bed, and it took her some time before she could drift off to sleep. Steve was still filling her mind with thoughts.

84

Steve left Leslie's with happy thoughts of her, too. He had had a marvelous evening. Just being with Leslie had seemed so right. She was someone special to him, and he knew he had always truly cared about her. He felt entirely different about her than any other girl he had dated. He wondered if this was love. He couldn't wait to make another date and see her again. She was so beautiful and natural—no put on about Leslie. He whistled a little tune as he got out of the car and went into the house. He really felt good, and he stretched contentedly as he lay in bed hoping he'd have good dreams of this lovely lady who was fast becoming very important to him.

Chapter 20

Bob and Mona were at a loss for words over Jacob's drinking and fighting problem. They both knew that Jake hadn't been home as often lately, but they had just thought it was that he had to study. Since he had never given them any trouble, they had just let him do his own thing. After all, he was twenty-two years old. Perhaps they hadn't given him the encouragement that he needed. During the past few years, they had been so involved with Leslie and her problems that they had just ignored Jake. Bob had tried to have a good man-to-man talk with Jake, but it didn't seem very satisfactory to either of them.

Of course, they went to court with Jake and felt a certain amount of relief when he only received a fine and a stern warning from the judge. It could have been a lot worse. They didn't really know what to say to Jake. He seemed so remote. In fact, Bob felt that he was somewhat to blame. He had expected so much from Jake and just took their father-son relationship for granted. He hadn't been as close to him as he should have been. He didn't even know very much about Jake's dreams and aspirations for the future. Leslie had always overshadowed Jake, and maybe he was finally rebelling and saying, "Hey! Look at me! I'm a person, too."

As they left the courthouse Bob put his arm around Jake's shoulder and said, "Son, I've let you down. Please give your mother and me a chance to make it up to you."

Tears came to Jake's eyes as he answered, "Dad, you and Mom didn't do anything. I don't know why I was drinking—just to be one of the guys, I guess. When this other fellow began making slurring remarks about Leslie, I just reacted. After all, she is my sister, and I love her very much."

By this time Mona was in tears, and she said, "Jake, I promise you we will always be here for you. Thank God everything turned out okay, and we'll all get a second chance." Jake stayed over one more day before having to go back to school, and he felt closer to his parents than he had in years. They talked about Leslie, and Mona told him that she was going out with Steve Malloy. Jake remembered Steve from high school, even though he was four years ahead of him. Steve had been

87

popular with both the girls and the boys in school, and Jake thought it was wonderful that he and Leslie were dating. Mona wondered if they had made a mistake in hiding the truth about Steve and the baby and her death. Not to know you had a beautiful niece who died, and that Steve was responsible. Well, it was too late now. The decision had been made long ago, and they would simply have to live with it.

The time Jake spent at home ended up being one of the nicest times they had had with him in a long time. They all relaxed and seemed to just enjoy being together. Jake had grown into such a handsome young man. They teased him about girls, and he finally admitted that he had gone out a few times with a girl in one of his classes. Her name was Emily Crawford, and she lived in one of the dormitories. She came from Ashville, a modest town about a hundred miles from Warren. Her dad was the sheriff of that county. Emily might never speak to him again if she heard what he'd done, that he'd been arrested for drinking and fighting. He hoped her dad didn't hear about it. The more Jake thought about it, the more ashamed he was. His folks had really been decent about the whole thing, although he knew that he had disappointed them. Actually, he had just been goofing off a lot lately. His grades were going down, and it was simply because he didn't pay attention and he didn't study. He really liked school, and he just didn't know why he had let this happen. One thing for sure, he was going to do better. No more of this playing around. This was his life and his future that he was messing up. It was certainly time to grow up and take some responsibility for the things he did. When Jake left to go back to Warren, he assured his mom and dad that he had learned his lesson and that they wouldn't have to worry about him anymore. As they waved goodbye, Mona and Bob had a good feeling that Jake meant what he said.

Chapter 21

When Joan took Tonya home, she was a little surprised at how abrupt Hannah was. She hurried Tonya inside and very quickly said good night. Mary Ann looked puzzled, too, and Joan had a strong feeling that things weren't right here. Tonya had said some disturbing things about her stepfather, Ralph, and she didn't seem to be too fond of him. Joan didn't notice any bruises on Tonya, but she got the idea that Tonya, and maybe Hannah, was a little afraid of him. Tonya and Mary Ann had had such a good time together, and Joan had wanted the chance to ask Hannah if they could do this again soon. Joan knew how much Mary Ann liked Tonya. She hadn't understood why a couple of weeks ago Many Ann didn't wear her new dress to a special program at school. Just the night before she had turned round and round in front of the mirror admiring herself. My, she looked nice. Joan had bought the dress especially for the program. Mary Ann's class was to sing, and Joan saw how excited she was to be performing. Mary Ann went upstairs to get dressed, but when she came down, she had on one of her regular school-day dresses. Joan was surprised and asked her why she wasn't wearing hew new dress. Mary Ann replied, "Mama, it's a beautiful dress, but Tonya won't have one, and I don't want her to feel bad." Joan hugged her and told her how nice she looked anyway. Mary Ann was such a sensitive child, so thoughtful and caring. Joan felt all choked up and warm inside just knowing that her beautiful little girl was also beautiful on the inside. After meeting Tonya, Joan began to understand how protective Mary Ann was of her.

Mary Ann's arm was giving her a little problem. Sometimes she just said it hurt, and she tried to be very careful in moving it. The doctor had prescribed some medicine for her if she had pain, but Mary Ann didn't want to take it. She said it made her feel funny, and Joan really didn't want her to unless it really became necessary. Even though the arm was bandaged and in a sling, there was still a certain amount of movement. Tonight had been great for Mary Ann having Tonya around. Tonya was almost the exact opposite of Mary Ann. She had shoulder-length dark hair and dark-brown eyes. Her skin was the color of a fresh suntan, and she had two dimples that she couldn't hide even if she was frowning. She was a sweet child, but sometimes her eyes gave off a look of fear, then she'd be all smiles again. When she spoke of "him," her stepfather, Ralph, Joan noticed this fearful look. She decided that one of these days soon she was going to visit Hannah again and see if she could find out what was going on. She had liked Hannah when they met, and Tonya was all smiles when she spoke lovingly of her mother. Joan shrugged and thought, I'm probably just imagining things and anyway it's none of my business. But not being any of her business had never stopped Joan before, and it was unlikely to this time.

When Hannah had Tonya inside and the door shut, she hugged her and told her she should do her homework and get ready for bed. Tonya said, "I've already done my homework. Mary Ann and I did it together." She longed to tell her everything about Mary Ann's house, her room and her mama and papa, but she could tell by Hannah's actions that Ralph was mad, so she said nothing.

Just as she started to her room, Ralph yelled for her to come to the living room where he was sprawled on the couch. Her heart sinking, she walked to where he was. His first words made her cringe. "Well, missy, I guess you think you're real smart not coming straight home from school. You know the rules. You don't need to go home with some rich kid. What do they see in you anyway? You have everything you need right here, don't you?" Tonya quickly nodded her head yes. "The next time you want to go someplace, you ask me, not your mother. She'd let you do anything. Now get to bed, and I'll be in to say good night." Tonya ran to her room, happy to be out of his sight, but knowing she had to go through the "goodnight" bit.

Hannah sat in the living room darning some socks and letting out the hem in another one of Tonya's dresses. My, she was growing fast. Ralph was watching television, but she knew that today's episode wasn't over. She hated to seem so rude to Mrs. Lambert and Mary Ann, but she couldn't bear for them to encounter Ralph. More and more lately she had known things were getting worse between herself and Ralph, and she finally had to face the fact that she was afraid of him. He had never really hit her, but he had pushed her more than once, and at these times she thought she saw an absolute look of hate on his face. He had screamed and yelled at Tonya, but he had never hit her. Hannah knew Tonya didn't like Ralph, but she never really talked about him at all.

Before her marriage to Ralph, Hannah had worked in the local telephone office. In fact, she would have loved to have continued working, but Ralph insisted that her place was at home with Tonya, although she had been in a lovely day-care center, and later to kindergarten and now first grade. This really left Hannah with a lot of time on her hands, but Ralph wouldn't even let her talk about going back to work. He wanted her at home. Hannah had lost touch with most of her friends after her marriage, and Ralph discouraged her from making new ones. It was as if she was his possession, and he didn't want to share her with anyone. She needed to talk to someone, but who?

Chapter 22

Hannah lay awake watching the clock long before the alarm sounded. She quickly jumped up, slipped into her robe, and hurried to the kitchen to put on the coffee and to make breakfast. As she came to Tonya's door, she slipped inside and shook the tiny shoulders and told her it was time to get up. Usually she just knocked on her way by, but she didn't want to make too much noise this morning. She felt terrible. She had tried to figure out what she was going to do with her life, but she was no nearer a solution than she was last night. She needed to talk to Ralph, but she knew that it would only set him off again.

She heard drawers being opened and shut from her bedroom, and she knew Ralph was up and getting ready for work. She had his lunch made—he insisted on taking his lunch—and his breakfast ready to be served. She never knew what kind of mood he would be in.

As Ralph came into the kitchen, she quickly poured him a cup of hot coffee and placed it in front of him. He stretched a little as he sat down, and a half smile played around his face. "I sure slept good last night. How about you?" he asked Hannah.

"Oh, I slept fine," she answered, silently thanking God that he seemed in a pretty good mood. She placed his eggs, bacon, and toast in front of him and then sat down to drink her coffee.

"Aren't you eating?" he asked.

"Oh yes," she said, "I'll eat with Tonya. I just wanted to sit here with you and have my coffee." She prayed that he would be gone before Tonya came in, but Ralph hollered from his chair for her to get in there. She'd had plenty of time to get dressed, he said. Tonya came in, looked up at her mom, and said, "I didn't quite finish my hair."

"I'll help you later," Hannah replied. "Just sit down now and have your breakfast."

Tonya slowly sipped her orange juice and waited as her mother jellied her toast and passed her a plate with an egg and bacon. She'd rather have had frosted flakes, but Ralph never let her have anything different from what he had. Only when he left early could she have anything she wanted. She picked at her food, hoping he'd leave before she had to eat it all.

Ralph looked at his watch, took his lunch box off the table, and started toward the door. Then he turned and said to Tonya, "Missy, you had better remember to get straight home from school today or you will be sorry, very sorry." As the door closed behind him Hannah breathed a sigh of relief. This house belonged to her. She had bought it with the insurance money from Tonya's dad, but how could she ever get Ralph out of it?

She quickly gave Tonya some frosted flakes and later helped her get her hair just right. She walked out the front door with her and gave her a big hug. She watched as Tonya skipped along to school.

As fast as she could, Hannah cleaned up the kitchen and then went to her room to get dressed. She had to talk to someone, but who? Things were getting worse, and she didn't know how long she could protect Tonya. To the outside world, Ralph was a steady, hard-working man. Any friends she had were Ralph's friends and any relative she had lived a long way off. She had really cut herself off from family when she married Ralph and moved to Warren. She was beside herself.

Just then the phone rang. The sound startled Hannah, and she hurried to answer it. From the other end she heard a voice saying, "This is Joan Lambert. I was wondering if I might come over and pick you up for lunch today. Our girls are so fond of each other that I think we should be friends."

Hannah burst into tears and said, "Oh Joan, please come over as soon as you can. I need someone to talk to—to help me."

Puzzled, Joan said, "Hannah, I'll be right over."

On the way over Joan kept wondering what could be wrong. That poor woman sounded desperate, she thought.

And at the Emersons' house, Hannah kept thinking as she hung up the phone. What have I done? This woman is a stranger, but maybe that was best. She had to talk to someone.

As soon as Tonya got to school, she looked for Mary Ann, and there she was—waiting for her. She had decided to ask Mary Ann about her papa. Mary Ann would tell her. There wasn't much time before school started, but she would have a good talk with her at recess. Hand in hand they went into the

94

classroom, and Tonya tried to concentrate on her work. It was hard though because she had so many things on her mind. She was worried, but she dismissed her bad thoughts and she'd wait until recess when she would tell everything to Mary Ann.

Hannah must have been watching for Joan, for the door seemed to open automatically. Hannah looked pale and extremely distressed. Joan hugged her and said, "Hannah, what's wrong? How can I help?" Hannah motioned her to the kitchen and poured them both a cup of coffee. The kitchen was a warm, cozy room. Gleaming copper pans hung behind the stove and short cottage curtains surrounded the window over the sink. It was a room made for confidences. Joan waited, letting Hannah lead the conversation. First Hannah thanked her for coming and apologized for her behavior the evening before. Finally, after much hesitation, she said, "Joan, I'm at my wit's end. I don't know what to do. My marriage is more like a prison and Ralph is the warden." She began by telling her how she had married Ralph, hoping to find the happiness she had had with her first husband. His illness had been lingering leukemia, but even then she had known how he loved her and baby Tonya, and she had wanted all that again. Her folks were against her marrying again, and they particularly didn't like Ralph. Hannah thought it could have been because she would be moving Tonya away from them, and although Ralph was very opinionated, he said he loved her, and how could anyone not love Tonya? She was such a good baby. When they had moved to Warren, Hannah had wanted to transfer from her job with the telephone company here, but Ralph was very adamant about her not working. He was the man of the house, and he would take care of them. Hannah remembered smiling to herself and thinking how protective Ralph was of her. They had looked around to buy a house, and when they found this one she was delighted. It wasn't a big fancy house, but a small comfortable one. It had a nice front porch where you could sit in the evenings and watch people go by and watch the children playing. It had three bedrooms, a nice light living room with two bay windows. She had made cushions so they became window seats. It even had a small laundry room and a fenced-in back yard. Of course, the kitchen was the hub of the house, warm, cozy, and intimate. Ralph had been hesitant at first. Oh, he liked the house, but the payments he thought might be too high. That was when Hannah decided to use her insurance money to buy the house. Never had she felt so good and secure as she did when the papers were all signed and the house was theirs. She was content at first just to be at home fixing up the house and taking care of Tonya, but later she began to feel cooped up. Ralph always wanted her at home. If he called and she wasn't there, he wanted to know why. Eventually, she came to feel that this house had become her prison.

She told Joan how strict Ralph was with Tonya and that even though they had the money, she wasn't allowed to buy anything for Tonya unless it was an absolute necessity. She explained why she had not invited them in last night and why she had so quickly closed the door. Ralph was mad and he could be nasty, and she was embarrassed for anyone to see what was happening. Hannah finally told Joan how last night Ralph had gone to kiss Tonya good night, and then when he came to bed he literally raped her.

Joan took her in her arms and said, "Oh, Hannah, you can't endure this. What can I do to help? This man is sick. He might hurt Tonya."

Hannah said, "That's what I'm afraid of. Up to now he's only pushed me around, and only shook Tonya a time or two, but things are getting worse. I want Ralph to get out, but I don't know what he will do if I tell him I want a divorce. I only have a little money that I put away for Tonya. I would need to get a job very soon, and that's scary. I only have telephone experience."

Joan's mind had been whirling. "Okay, first things first. I know a good lawyer that can help, Peter Magness. He's an old friend of mine and Paul's. I'll take you to see him this morning. Second, Tonya cannot be in the house when you confront Ralph, but that's no problem. I'll take her home with me. I need to use your phone to call Peter, and we will go and see him to see what he recommends."

At recess, as soon as they went outside to the playground, Tonya said, "Mary Ann, I want to ask you something. Does your papa come to your room and kiss you good night?"

"Sure," Mary Ann said, "not always to my room. Sometimes we kiss good night when I go to my room."

96

Tonya said, "Does your papa ever rub around on you like under your gown?"

"Oh no," Mary Ann answered. "No one is supposed to touch you down there. My mama explained that to me."

Tonya said, "Ralph does that to me, and I don't like it at all, but I'm afraid if I tell Mama, he'll hurt me. He told me never to tell."

Mary Ann hugged Tonya as she started to cry. "Don't cry, Tonya. I'll tell my mama. She'll know what to do." Tonya dried her eyes, and she felt better. Mary Ann was her very best friend, and she could trust her.

Chapter 23

Leslie had worked hard this week. It seemed there were more accidents, more babies, and more sick people. She loved to be busy, and it was always a "good tiredness" when she went to bed at night. She'd been waiting patiently to hear from Steve, and now that she had made another date with him she could hardly wait. She went over and over again in her mind the St. Patrick's Day party and finally came to the conclusion that Steve was entirely a different person now. He was no longer that cocky college boy who was just looking for a good time. He was a mature, caring, sensitive man. Leslie had already made up her mind to forget all the past and concentrate on the future. Steve might well be a part of that future. She knew that when she was with Steve, she felt all tingly and content and safe and loving. In spite of the past, she felt he could be trusted to look out for her. She knew she spent lots of time thinking about Steve, and conjuring up his face anytime made her smile. His was such a handsome face. The remains of the scars just gave him character. She had been especially bright and cheerful today. Even Dr. Evans remarked to her as she accompanied him on his rounds, "Leslie, you act like someone in love. Is he anyone I know?" She laughed and said, "Oh, doctor, you're such a romantic. I'm just going out with Steve Malloy again. We've known each other since high school." He gave her one of those "knowing" looks, but didn't say anything else. He did know that whatever was on Leslie's mind was good for her. He'd never seen her so pepped up.

When Steve arrived that night, Leslie was all ready to go. As a matter of fact she had been ready at least a half hour early. She wasn't sure she understood how she felt. She was all breathless and couldn't get the picture of Steve out of her head. She was as giddy as a schoolgirl, and here she was going on twenty-five years old. She smiled as she opened the door, and Steve let out a low whistle. "You look ravishing," he said. Leslie blushed a little. She had deliberately made herself as "ravishing" as possible, and apparently her efforts had paid off. She was wearing a rose-colored dress with a scalloped low-cut neckline (lower than normal for her) that showed the soft rounds of her breasts. The fitted bodice emphasized her small waist, going into a flared skirt. She wore her pearl earrings and a single choker of pearls around her neck. They were only going out to dinner and she had probably overdressed, but it certainly felt good seeing his eyes light up as he looked at her. This time Steve told her he had selected a new restaurant in town which also had a small dance floor. This sounded great to Leslie, and she was all smiles as Steve helped her into his car. The evening could not have gone better. The prime rib was cooked to perfection, and Steve had ordered a glass of red wine to accompany it. Leslie didn't ordinarily drink, and she was a little surprised until Steve assured her that this was a special occasion. She sipped the wine slowly, not sure whether she liked it or not. In college, Leslie had tried beer and a few mixed drinks, but she didn't care for them at all, and not having grown up around alcohol she hadn't felt the need to explore it further. Alcohol was what the local drunks imbibed in, and nice Christian folks didn't drink. She'd never truly thought about it too much. It did bring to mind the night of the St. Patrick's Day party and the trips Steve kept making outside to drink from the hidden flasks. Later after they had eaten all they possibly could and sat sipping coffee, Steve asked her to dance. The only other time she had danced with Steve was at the party, and this was entirely different. As Steve put his arms around her, she felt all nervous and giddy, and she wanted just to hold him more tightly to her. She nestled her head against his shoulder and let the soft music envelope her. She didn't ever want the music to end, but of course it did. Her feelings for Steve were like none other she had ever experienced, and she was confused. When the music ended and they went back to their table, Steve said, "Leslie, let's get out of here."

When they were seated back in the car, Steve hesitated before starting the engine, and he faced Leslie, saying, "I don't know where to begin, but I am falling in love with you. In fact, I may have loved you ever since our first date years ago. I've been afraid to kiss you or touch you, afraid you would reject me after the way I behaved before. Believe me, Leslie, when I tell you again how sorry I am and that I would never repeat such actions again. Can you forgive me and trust me and care about me?"

Leslie didn't know what to say. Her heart was beating

fast, almost singing. Dare she admit that she loved him, too? How would her folks react to that? She just placed her arms around his neck and moved her lips slowly up to cover his. Steve groaned and pulled her to him as their mouths joined in a hunger that both of them wanted. Breathlessly they finally parted, and Steve continued to kiss her face and her eyes, stroking her hair and murmuring her name over and over. Leslie didn't know how long they sat in the parking lot kissing and discovering one another. She did finally know that it was time to go, and reluctantly Steve started the engine. They spoke little on the way to Leslie's, each consumed by the enormity of what they had discovered and admitted—that they were in love. For Steve, he was elated and the solution was simple. They would get married and live happily ever after. He had a good job. He could afford a family, and his mom and dad already loved Leslie. For her it was very complicated. Her dad, particularly, never had forgiven Steve for what happened before, and there was no way she could tell Steve about Angel. What could a relationship ever be without trust and honesty? If she told Steve about Angel, she could lose him. He could hate her for not telling him before, and if she didn't tell him, she would be living a lie. She was, to say the least, confused.

When they reached Leslie's house, Steve took her hand and asked, "Leslie, will you marry me? I know this may seem sudden to you, but it really isn't. I've waited all my life for you."

Leslie gulped back her tears and said, "Steve, I do love you, but I must have time to think. There are so many things to consider. My career, my family, your obligations to your parents. I don't want us to get carried away with the moment. We're talking about the rest of our lives here. For me, marriage is forever. We both have to be very sure."

Steve could have wished to hear nothing but yes! yes!, but he understood where she was coming from. "You are right, Leslie. I'm sure I want to marry you, have children with you, and spend the rest of my life making you happy. I also know that you must feel the same way, and this is all new to you. I won't rush you, but I'll never give up hoping you will say yes."

He came around to open the door for her, and she reached out to touch his face and gave him a quick kiss. She

101

said, "Let me go by myself. I need some time to think." And with that she hurried inside. Already she knew she'd never be able to sleep. Yes, she loved Steve, but how could she find the solution to all the problems?

Chapter 24

After listening to Hannah's description of Ralph's behavior, Peter Magness felt that this woman had really only touched the surface of what this man was capable of. He asked Hannah if she was sure she was ready to tackle a divorce. It could be a nasty situation, although he assured her that she certainly had ample reason to wish to dissolve this marriage. Ralph had never adopted Tonya even though she used his name at school, so she would not be an issue. The house, although it was paid for by Hannah, could cause problems.

Peter suggested that Hannah tell Ralph, this evening if possible, that she wanted a divorce, and if necessary they could get a restraining order to keep him away from the house. The whole thing frightened Hannah, and she wasn't sure she could be strong enough to stand up to Ralph. Joan and Peter both told her they would support her actions, and Hannah realized that she had no other choice if she ever wanted to have a life.

On the way home from Peter's office, Joan and Hannah made plans. Joan would take Tonya's clothes home with her, and she would pick Tonya up at school along with Mary Ann. Joan promised to help Hannah look for a job and left her at her house with Hannah's promise to call her whatever the time, and she'd be there for her.

After Joan left, Hannah began to shake and had to lie down. She was afraid of Ralph. No matter how she had tried to fool herself before, she never knew what Ralph would do next. She made herself a cup of tea and tried to pull her thoughts together. She thought of David, her first husband, and how gentle he was. This was the kind of man she wanted and needed. Ralph was unkind and mean. Everything was a possession for Ralph, and she finally had to admit that Ralph had always resented Tonya. He had never loved her. How could she have been so blind? She knew that she had to talk to Ralph as soon as he came home. No matter how afraid she was, she had to do it.

Joan picked up Mary Ann and when she told Tonya that her mother had given permission for her to spend the night with Mary Ann, she looked puzzled. "But Ralph said I couldn't go anywhere without asking him first." Tonya said. Joan assured her that this time it was okay and that she already had taken her school clothes for the next day home with her. Mary Ann was delighted, but Tonya still had that apprehensive look on her face.

Riding home, Mary Ann said, "Oh, Mama, Ralph does bad things to Tonya when he kisses her good night."

"What things, Tonya?" Joan asked.

Before Tonya could reply, Mary Ann said, "Mama, he puts his hand in her panties."

Joan gasped. "My God, what is this man capable of?" Her mind was whirling as she pulled into the driveway. She took Tonya's hand and said, "You can tell me everything when we get inside." The girls put up their books, and Joan sat down on the sofa, a girl on each side. With her arms hugging her, Tonya told Joan how Ralph breathed hard on her and how bad he smelled and how he had put his hands under her gown and felt around. She didn't like it, but Ralph told her she'd be very sorry if she told her mom or anyone. She was obviously frightened now that she had told. "Don't worry, Tonya, we won't let Ralph hurt you. You did right to tell Mary Ann and me." She took the girls to the kitchen, gave them some milk and cookies, and then went as fast as she could to the phone. She had to tell Peter. This certainly put a new light on things. He'd know how and when they could tell Hannah.

When Peter heard everything, he was thankful that Tonya was with Joan. He had to talk to Hannah before Ralph got home. He didn't even know how safe Hannah would be alone with Ralph. If she wanted him to, he could be there when she confronted Ralph. This man was sexually abusing his six-year-old stepdaughter. That was the long and short of it. He called Hannah, and she said she was expecting Ralph in about an hour and a half. Peter didn't explain on the phone, but he said, "Hannah, I'm coming over. I have some things to tell you, and I'll be with you when you speak to Ralph."

After she hung up the telephone, Hannah began to be more and more frightened. Peter sounded real serious, and maybe it would be better if her lawyer was there when she told him she wanted a divorce. She was looking out the window when she saw Peter drive up and rushed to open the door for him. She took one look at Peter's grim face and said, "What is it? What's wrong?"

104

There was no easy way to tell her, so he looked her right in the eyes and said, "Hannah, Ralph has been sexually abusing Tonya."

Hannah felt all her blood rushing to her head, and Peter had to hold her to keep her from falling. "Oh God, how could this be? Peter, how do you know?" A million questions came to mind. Ralph had come to bed last night, fully aroused, and raped her, and he had come straight from Tonya's room. How could she have been so blind and stupid? Peter went on to tell her how Tonya had first told Mary Ann and then Joan. Hannah was no longer afraid of Ralph. A cold rage settled over her, and she knew that Ralph would be out of her house today. Peter calmed her down, but he readily recognized that this was not the frightened person he had met earlier today, but a strong, determined mother who would protect her child. He didn't envy anyone who got in her way.

When Ralph came in the door, he saw Peter, and a frown crossed his face. "Who are you?" he asked.

Hannah said quietly, "Ralph, this is Mr. Peter Magness, my lawyer. He is here at my request. I want a divorce, and I'd like you to take your personal things and leave this house in the next few hours." Ralph's face turned from white to red, and he started toward Hannah until he saw the look on Peter's face. Ralph began his name calling of Hannah and told her that she could get out, he wasn't going anywhere. Hannah listened in silence until he stopped for a breath, and then she said quite calmly, "You will go, Ralph, and never come back, or you will be in jail for sexually abusing my child. I could endure your treatment of me, even excuse your behavior, but not this. You are a sick man, and I want you away from Tonya and me forever. Mr. Magness is here to see that happen. You can go quietly, or the police can help you. You will have the divorce papers in a few days, and there will be a restraining order keeping you away from this house, Tonya, and me."

Ralph was in a rage, but he had never seen that mousy wife of his like this before. She was standing up to him, no sign of fright. He'd like to squash her like a big bug. He felt a hardness beginning in his groin. This was the kind of woman he'd like to show a thing or two in bed. He would, too, if that nosy lawyer wasn't here. He went to his bedroom, took down a bag, and began putting his clothes in it. He kept wondering where that little brat was. He had told her to keep her mouth shut. When he saw her, she'd pay and pay good for this. He gathered up his toilet articles, zipped up his bag, and went to the living room where Hannah and Peter were waiting. She might think she had the upper hand, but she was wrong. No sir, no dumb broad was going to throw him out.

As he passed through the door, he assured Hannah that she hadn't seen the last of him. Peter called to him, "Mr. Emerson, I suggest you get your own lawyer and stay away from this house. It will be in your best interest to allow your lawyer to handle everything for you. The law does not look kindly on child molesting."

Ralph mumbled as he got in his car and drove away. He'd show that Mister Smart Lawyer. Even though he talked big, deep down he felt the gnawing feeling of fear slowly tying his guts in knots. If that little brat had kept her mouth shut like he'd told her to do . . . He hadn't really hurt her any, just a little feeling around.

He didn't know where he was going—the YMCA, he guessed. At least for tonight until he could work something out tomorrow.

After Ralph left, Hannah sank down on the sofa. She was exhausted and at the same time relieved. Peter prepared to leave, and he advised Hannah to keep the door bolted, just in case Ralph decided to come back. He was glad he had been there for Hannah. Ralph was a violent man. It was easily seen in his actions tonight. The fact that they knew about him molesting Tonya was the deciding factor in Ralph's leaving. When he had a chance to talk to Tonya, he would probably advise Hannah to notify the police and allow them to prosecute him. He felt they were both safe for the moment.

She thanked Peter over and over for being there, and when he left she followed his advice. She bolted the doors (although Ralph had keys) and went to the phone to call Joan and tell her what had happened. She wanted to hear Tonya's voice, too. Hannah felt so guilty. She was Tonya's mother and hadn't recognized the signs of what was happening. After talking to Joan and saying good night to Tonya, Hannah hung up the phone and thought about trying to eat something. She didn't feel hungry, but she knew she had a lot ahead of her and she couldn't afford to be sick. She put on the kettle for a cup of tea and opened a can of soup. Thank heavens, she had the good sense to put the balance of her insurance money in a certificate with her name and Tonya's on it. At least Ralph couldn't touch it. She never had much cash, however. She had tried to save every week from the grocery money Ralph gave her. That was the only way she could get things for Tonya. She checked her "hidey hole," and she had a little over four hundred dollars. She'd have to find a job fast, and she'd have to get some kind of car. Ralph had always said she didn't need one. He'd take her where she needed to go.

She rolled and tumbled in bed, and at one-thirty she was still begging for sleep. Finally the dark curtain of night fell around her, and as the clock struck three A.M., she fell into a dreamless sleep.

Chapter 25

Mona was still distressed after her lengthy phone conversation with Leslie. As a matter of fact, she had been stunned. She knew Leslie had been seeing Steve, but she never dreamed it would become serious. Mona was still tied in knots over seeing the Lambert child, not knowing whether she should pursue her suspicions or not. She hadn't told anyone except Dr. Williams, and he obviously didn't believe her. Now this. Leslie had said she hadn't given Steve an answer yet, but she did admit that she cared very much for him. Actually, she and Bob had liked Steve, and he came from a good family. The only thing hanging over their heads was baby Angel. She was gone now, and there was really no reason to dredge up the past. On this she agreed with Leslie. Even so, a part of her kept thinking that between a husband and wife there had to be trust and honesty. Only three people in the family knew about the baby, and of course there were hospital records. They had kept the secret for six years; why not forever? At this point she didn't know if Leslie would say yes to Steve. Bob hadn't had too much to say about it. Leslie was his little girl, and he just wanted her to be happy. The past was the past, and he could put it to rest forever. Leslie was going on twenty-five years old, and she would have to decide for herself if Steve was the man she wanted to spend the rest of her life with or not. He knew Mona had been upset lately. She had passed it off as nothing, but he knew that sooner or later she'd tell him. He smiled a little to himself. He knew Mona so well. She always ended up telling him her little secrets. Actually, they had never been able to keep secrets from one another. They had never wanted to, each needing the comfort and understanding of the other.

Leslie was still in a turmoil. She loved Steve, and she wanted to say yes. She had talked to him on the phone, but hadn't seen him since the night he proposed. He had called her early the next morning after their date. He just wanted to hear her voice. Leslie had wanted to say yes then, but she had to talk to her parents, and she had to get things clear in her own mind. One minute she would decide to tell Steve everything, the next minute cold terror that she would lose him if she told him gripped her. She knew her dad's feelings. Let sleeping dogs lie, and maybe he was right. Nothing could be changed, and she was getting on with her life pretty well.

Tonight was the big night. Tonight she would give Steve her answer. She began to realize more and more how much she loved him, and like Steve had said, it may have really started back years ago. In the past few years, she had never truly been attracted to anyone, but with Steve, it was different. When Steve came tonight she was going to say "yes" and never look back. She knew her parents would do whatever she wanted them to. She felt light and gay and happy now that she had finally settled everything in her mind. Actually, she could hardly wait until time to go home and time for Steve to arrive. She was walking on clouds, and although she had worked really hard today, she didn't even feel tired. Love can do wonders, she thought laughingly to herself. Dr. Evans had been right—she was in love.

When Steve finally arrived, Leslie was suddenly calm when she saw him. This was the man she wanted to spend the rest of her life with. He was looking at her with the same intensity. They both knew at that moment that their destiny was one and the same. Leslie stood in the shelter of his arms and said, "Yes, Steve, I'll marry you. You are the man I want to live my whole life with."

He kissed her then, and when they finally parted, he pulled a small velvet box out of his pocket. "I just knew the answer had to be yes," he said, "so I have this for you—an engagement ring." Leslie gasped as she viewed the emerald cut diamond solitaire ring as it flashed its signals of love and hope in the light. Steve slipped the ring on her finger and said, "Leslie, I promise to love you all my life." After a lingering kiss of promise, they just hugged and laughed and were as giddy as a couple of teenagers. They wanted to hold each other and talk and make plans. Now that they were officially engaged, they wanted to tell everyone.

Leslie wanted to call her parents first, and when Mona answered she could hear the excitement in Leslie's voice. It didn't matter that she might have misgivings and a lot of unanswered questions. She had to be happy for her daughter. She and Bob both offered their congratulations, and they promised to see them over the weekend to discuss wedding plans. No, they hadn't set the date yet, but they both knew they wanted it soon. Jacob was delighted when Leslie called him. Now he'd have a big brother.

When Steve called his parents, they were very happy. They had known Leslie for a long time. She was Peggy's friend. They weren't even surprised. They had seen the look on Steve's face every time he looked at Leslie. Peggy had known her brother pretty well, and she had sensed the feelings between Steve and Leslie when Steve had his accident. They were very happy for the young couple and wanted to be in on all of the wedding plans.

After the calls had been made, they started talking about the wedding. Steve wanted it to be right away and so did Leslie, but they both knew that their parents expected a big wedding and needed time to prepare for it. Their love could wait a little longer, and even though Leslie would have been happy with a simple ceremony, Steve knew that every girl deserved a beautiful wedding day to cherish forever, and at this point he would deny Leslie nothing.

They had planned to go out tonight, but they were both too excited to think of eating, perhaps a little later. Right now they just wanted to relish the moment of their delight and of their love.

When would the wedding be? They wanted to be married before Christmas, and that was only a little over two months away. When could Leslie get leave from the hospital for at least a short honeymoon? Was two months long enough for the mothers of the bride and groom to plan a wedding? They looked at the calendar and decided that Friday, December 15, would be the day. This would allow them a short honeymoon and to still be home with their families for Christmas. They both realized it would be a long wait for them, but then they would have all the rest of their lives.

By nine-thirty they decided it was time to get something to eat, and anyway Leslie wanted to show off her new ring. They were bursting to shout their good news to everyone they saw. How little they realized that their happiness and love for each other literally glowed from their faces. Leslie and Steve were engaged, and they were going to be married on December 15. No two people were ever happier than they were at this very moment.

Chapter 26

Peter Magness leaned back in his chair and gazed out the window. He had a nice view from his second-story office, but it wasn't the view he was thinking about. It was Hannah Emerson he had on his mind this morning. It had been almost a month since she had first come to his office and two weeks since she had started working as his receptionist, secretary, and general assistant. She had been reluctant at first when he offered her the job. She wasn't qualified, she said, as a lawyer's secretary. The woman who had worked for him wanted to go and spend some time with her daughter who was having a baby. This left him without anyone, and Hannah desperately needed a job. As far as he was concerned, it was working out beautifully. Hannah was a fast learner, and around people she seemed to come alive. Now that she was no longer a prisoner of Ralph's, the kind, sincere, and caring personality came through. Ralph had tried to give her a problem, but she had held her ground, along with a restraining order, and he had stayed away. Her divorce was granted two days ago, and now she just had a waiting period. She had been able to keep the house, and of course she'd asked for nothing more. She had said she really didn't know what Ralph's finances were. He had handled all the money himself, but she suspected it wasn't much, and she did have the money she had put up for Tonya. Now that she had a job, her immediate needs were taken care of. Peter and Hannah both had talked to Tonya about Ralph and came to the conclusion that Tonya had told Mary Ann in time, before any permanent damage had been done. Since Ralph had been gone, Tonya, like Hannah, had become a new person. She and Mary Ann were almost inseparable. Joan or Paul picked up both girls from school, and Hannah picked up Tonya on her way home from work. So far this had been a good arrangement for all of them. Peter began to think it had been his lucky day when Joan had brought Hannah to see him. He had been friends with Joan and Paul for a lot of years. They had first met while he was in Law School and was involved with one of Joan's friends. Just when they were about to announce their engagement, she ran off with someone else. It had taken him quite a long time to get over her and to salvage his pride. In fact, he swore off of women, and outside of casual dating, he had never succumbed to any feminine wiles again. He decided he was a dyed-in-the-wool bachelor, and often times his ego was boosted when he knew some young lady was vying for his attentions. He often envied some of his friends who had families, all the things he had believed he would one day have. Still, he wasn't too unhappy with his own life. He had a lucrative and satisfying business. He had his own house and a housekeeper who took care of it for him. He played golf on weekends and participated in Little League baseball in the summers. Yes, he had a lot to be thankful for, and it looked like he was going to have to add Hannah to that list. She'd certainly changed the atmosphere around the office.

For Hannah, Peter Magness had been a godsend. He had advised her as her lawyer and helped her get through the divorce from Ralph with less problems than she anticipated. Ralph's threats in the beginning so far had been just threats. The restraining order keeping him away from her and Tonya and the house had worked. Ralph was still unsure what was going to happen about his molesting Tonya, so he was staying quiet and out of the picture. Hannah had begun to realize more and more what a hold Ralph had had over her. It was hard for her to even imagine that she had let this happen to herself. All she wanted was a loving husband and to make a home for Tonya. Apparently she couldn't have a man in her life, but she could be happy with Tonya.

She had been afraid at first, when Peter offered her a job, that she couldn't do what he needed, but she soon found out that she seemed to fit right in. She had her own desk in the small but adequate reception area, and she had a sympathetic ear for all of the ones looking for legal help from Peter. When she didn't understand some of the legal terms in writing letters, Peter took time to explain them to her. She actually was beginning to feel like she knew what she was doing. Peter's office was homey. One could feel comfortable there. The two big easy chairs pulled up in front of his desk seemed to be waiting for you to leave your troubles. The view was not spectacular. It simply overlooked the hustle and bustle of a small city. It just lifted you up above the everyday comings and goings as if you were suspended in midair just looking in. The scene below was constantly changing, so you could never be bored. Peter declared his best "thinking" took place from his chair, just looking out.

Hannah had brought a lovely peace lily and placed it close to the window. She had also brought one for the reception room. To her all the rooms lacked was a green symbol of growing hope. Nothing could lift your spirits better than a nice plant. Actually, Hannah didn't know what she would ever have done without Joan and Professor Paul (she always thought of him as professor) and that lovely child, Mary Ann. She was so sensitive and caring. She could certainly understand why Tonya considered her her best friend. Now that Tonya could have friends over (Ralph never allowed it), Mary Ann had been able to spend the night, and Tonya was delighted. She was always glad to spend the night at the Lamberts,' but she also liked sharing her things with Mary Ann. Hannah hadn't been able to buy a lot of things for Tonya yet. She had bills to pay, and she bought a used car, but little by little she would get Tonya new clothes and finally get rid of some of the dresses with the white crease around the bottom. Tonya was growing so fast that she was outgrowing most everything anyway. Things were really looking up for Hannah, and for the first time since David died, she began to feel that she was somebody and that she was a whole, worthwhile person again. A lot of the credit she gave to Peter Magness.

Chapter 27

Everyone wanted in on planning the wedding, and Leslie thought she'd go nuts listening to all the suggestions. Of course, it was in fun because the real planning was taking place between Mona and Steve's mom, Norma. Occasionally she and Steve would be asked to give an opinion, most often discarded after it was offered. Leslie had vetoed six bridesmaids, saying instead that she wanted Peggy to be matron of honor, and Alice and Beverly from the hospital to be bridesmaids. Steve had asked his dad to be best man and chose Jake and Peggy's husband, Jack, for groomsmen. They didn't want a big wedding, but both Leslie and Steve had grown up in Evanston where everybody knew everything about everyone else. They couldn't leave out anyone. As plans progressed, both Leslie and Steve thought eloping would have been the simplest plan. It was exciting and great fun if they survived. A December wedding. What color for the bridesmaids' dresses? A lush forest green of crushed velvet with a scalloped neckline and puffed sleeves. A fitted bodice with a full skirt, ballerina length, a wide sash to encircle the waist, tied in a big bow in the back. The dresses looked simple, but the material added the elegance. All agreed it was an excellent choice. They would wear pumps dyed to match. The groomsmen would all wear their own suits. The minister had been selected, and the local Baptist church had been reserved for December 15.

Now to find Leslie a dress. She visited bridal shop after bridal shop and tried on many beautiful dresses. Some didn't feel right on, others were too expensive. She really wanted a simple one, but with elegance as well. Finally, she saw it. Just the one she wanted in a shop window. It was a satin fitted bodice flowing into a flared skirt. The neckline was v-shaped and covered with tiny seed pearls. The sleeves were leg-of-mutton, the same pattern of pearls decorating the arms. A long train fell from the waist. When Leslie stepped into this creation, she felt every bit the bride. The dress fit like a glove, and she knew she would not look further. She selected a beaded halo from which fell a shoulder-length veil. She wanted to show the dress to Steve, but Mona and Norma insisted that she wait for him to see it as she walked down the aisle. It was sure to be bad luck for him to see it before. As the day drew nearer and nearer, Leslie couldn't keep her head out of the clouds. Her friends at work had given her a lingerie shower, and even Dr. Chris had kept giving her that knowing eye. She took a lot of good-natured teasing at work, and even a few of her patients mentioned the glow and ever-ready smile she had. She was glad she had Mona and Norma to take care of all the details, flowers, cake, getting the invitations out. Of course, everyone in Evanston was invited, and individual invitations were sent only to out-of-town people. The local newspaper had given an invitation notice to everyone when it had printed the picture of Steve and Leslie announcing their wedding plans. Leslie's dress was taken to her old room at home. This is where she would dress. Even though Leslie and Jacob both lived away from home in Warren, this house began to take on a festive air. Gifts were being delivered here, and with Norma's help, Mona was trying to decorate for Christmas. It was an exciting, hectic time. Steve would certainly be glad when this wedding was over. He never got to see Leslie alone anymore, but he never saw her more alive and beautiful, and he felt so happy he could burst. He had been in charge of the honeymoon plans. He really didn't care where they went. He just wanted to have Leslie all to himself. He would have loved to have whisked her away to some magical island, but he knew they would only have a week. They both wanted to be back home with their families for the holidays. He had thought about a secluded ski lodge in Colorado, but neither of them skied and a honeymoon was no time to learn. He also knew that he needed to find a place that wasn't all that expensive. Bob and Jim had both offered to finance their honeymoon, but Steve was reluctant to accept such help. While he was still pondering what they would do, Bob and Jim came with two tickets in hand for Hawaii. Both agreed they had never been, but it had to be the perfect honeymoon place. Steve was flabbergasted. He never expected this. Leslie would really be excited to be going to Hawaii. They had made reservations for them at the Outrigger Waikiki right on the beach. They would leave right after the wedding and fly home on December 23. Everything seemed perfect. The wedding was being held at 10:30 A.M. This would make it perfect for their flight.

The rehearsal night was finally over. Everything went wrong, and it was a good thing they had their dinner first. No one could have eaten after all the confusion of rehearsing. The soloist couldn't get through her song without sobbing, and nobody could decide where the mothers and the fathers should be seated, and in general everyone was tense and nervous. They tried to console one another by saying rehearsals were always like this so the wedding would be perfect.

When Leslie said good night to Steve, she tried to put on a brave face. As they kissed good night, they both knew the next time they saw each other they would be in church, and the next time they kissed they would belong to each other. They were glad the wedding was in the morning. They didn't think they could stand being apart much longer.

The morning finally came, and as Leslie opened her eyes, she was fully aware that this was the most important day of her life. It scared her a little. Yes, she loved Steve, and she wanted to marry him, but in the way back of her mind, the old doubts came flooding out to haunt her. She didn't have long to ponder, until Mona was knocking at her door, being sure she was awake and urging her to come to breakfast. Butterflies in her stomach didn't suggest food, but she did want some coffee and maybe some toast and juice would get her stomach settled. She had heard of bride's jitters, but she hadn't expected to feel this way. It was only seven-thirty, but she felt like it would take her forever to get ready for the big event. Jacob, Mona, and Bob were all waiting for her, smiling at her nervousness. Mona assured her she had plenty of time and her clothes were all laid out ready for her to step into them. Her going-away suit was at the church (she would change there) and her bags were already loaded in Steve's car for the honeymoon. The reception would be held in the church fellowship hall. Not only cake and punch, but a buffet of finger foods since it would be lunch time by the time the ceremony was finished, and this would give everyone a good chance to greet the bride and groom.

Leslie hurried from her shower so she'd have time for Mona to help with her hair. She wanted to pull it up in the back with a few tendrils hanging on the sides. Her headdress would sit better that way and allow the shine of her hair to glow through the veil. Mona went to dress while Leslie applied her

119

make-up and then she would help her into her beautiful wedding dress. It was arranged for Jacob and Mona to leave for the church a little before Leslie and Bob. That way Mona could check everything and see that all was well before Leslie arrived with her father—ready to walk down the aisle. The bridesmaids were dressing at the church, but all had agreed Leslie would dress at home with Mona's help, and this would give mother and daughter a few last minutes of quality time.

When the dress was finally zipped and the veil placed on her head, Mona's eyes filled with tears. This was her baby and the most beautiful bride she had ever seen. She quickly wiped her eyes and said, "Leslie, these are tears of joy. You are about to embark on the greatest adventure of your life. Always remember, 'to thine own self be true.' Just remember this day and know that you will always be my little girl, and I will always be there for you." With a quick hug, Mona went out the door where Jacob was waiting for her. Leslie looked around her room and knew that this room would never be the same for her again. When she returned, she would be a married woman.

Chapter 28

Leslie took a last look at herself in the mirror and knew it was time to leave with her dad for the church. She checked again, something old—the pearl earrings of Mona's. Also something borrowed, and something new—the beautiful string of pearls Steve had given her last night. Something blue—the garter she was wearing. At the last minute Jacob had given her a shiny penny to put in her shoe, for luck, he said. Bob helped to get her tucked in the car, and they drove slowly the few blocks to the church. There was a really big crowd. The parking areas were full. Of course, a place in front had been saved for the bride's car.

Mona had hurried ahead with Jacob to check everything. She wanted to be sure all the flowers were in place in the church and that everyone had the right corsage or boutonniere. She had to watch for Bob to be sure he had his in place. Norma was in charge of seeing to everything in the fellowship hall. Mona also had Leslie's bouquet, a small cluster of red rosebuds intertwined with baby's breath. She patted her hair, made sure her own corsage was firmly in place, took a last look in the sanctuary, and then went to the side door to wait for Bob and Leslie to arrive.

Steve was waiting in the minister's office with his dad, Jake, and Jack. It seemed he had been waiting for hours. This was it. The time for running was now or never. In the next hour he would have committed his life to join forever with another. He loved Leslie. He wanted to marry her, but he readily admitted to himself that he was scared. Jake and Jack were laughing and talking, but he was the one being led to slaughter! He swallowed a couple of times, almost sure he was going to throw up. Oh, what was that? The minister had asked him something about the ring. He thought his dad had it. Steve fumbled in his pocket, but his dad with a knowing look said, "Don't worry, Steve. I have the ring." He wondered if it would be okay if he sat down for a minute. It seemed awfully hot in there.

The bridesmaids, along with Norma, were all dressed and ready. They admired each other and peeked out to see what a large crowd was already in the church. They would each carry a long-stemmed red rose. Norma's dress was a teal-blue crepe

121

with raglan sleeves. It hung straight with an overblouse effect across the hips. She wore a gold locket that Jim had given her when they were married. Her corsage was white. Mona had chosen a mauve silk shirtwaist dress. The color was good for her, and the style accented a very young figure. Her corsage was white.

Jacob and Jack went out front to seat the guests, and Steve knew the time was getting near. He wondered what Leslie was thinking. What if she didn't show up? Maybe she'd changed her mind. The minister was touching his arm and saying, "It's time to go, Steve." He momentarily closed his eyes, said a little prayer, and forced himself to follow his dad and the minister to the altar where he faced a roomful of smiling faces.

On the way to the church Leslie and Bob had a little time to talk. Bob told her how much he loved her and that he would be there for her. He admitted that he did like Steve and that all he wanted was for the two of them to be happy. Bob helped her out of the car, and there was Mona waiting with her bouquet. Mona quickly put Bob's boutonniere on his coat, and she squeezed Leslie's hand just before starting into the church to be seated by Jacob. It was time.

Leslie had heard soft music being played as she arrived, but now as she clutched her father's arm, she was waiting for the wedding march. She saw Beverly go in and then Peggy. Next it would be her turn. She had a lot of mixed feelings; she was nervous and apprehensive. Was this the right thing to do? There it was—the music that announced the bride. She exhaled a deep breath, and she and Bob took the first steps. The church was so full, there were beautiful flowers, and then she saw him and everything else paled by comparison. There was this magnificent man, soon to be her husband, waiting at the altar for her. No longer did she have any doubts or misgivings. She knew that this man was the one she wanted to spend the rest of her life with.

As the wedding march began, Steve looked and saw this vision coming down the aisle. Never had he seen anyone so beautiful. The butterflies were gone, and any doubts he may have had were all swept away as Leslie came closer and closer. He was calm and ready to claim this woman to be his forever.

The ceremony was beautiful, and there was hardly a dry

eye when at last Steve kissed his bride, and they started their walk back down the aisle. Leslie's only regret was that her grandparents couldn't come. Papaw had been sick, and, of course, Mamaw wouldn't leave him. She had talked to both of them the day before and knew that they were with her in spirit. Both of her other grandparents, Bob's parents, had been dead for several years.

There was lots of picture taking, and then they went into the reception to cut the cake and greet all of their friends. Everyone was laughing and talking, and Steve was secretly hoping this wouldn't last too long so he could have his beautiful bride all to himself. The plans were all set to go to the airport, leave their car there, and go on to Hawaii for a short honeymoon. Bob and Jim had made all these arrangements for them. Everything was perfect.

After the cake was cut, the bouquet thrown, Leslie's garter thrown, the buffet eaten, Leslie went to change out of her wedding dress. She slipped out of it carefully, lovingly feeling the satin and the tiny pearls. She would save this dress for her daughter one day. A brief glimpse of Angel crossed her mind, but she knew she and Steve would have other children. Angel was on another time—gone forever.

Through showers of rice and cries from well-wishers, Leslie and Steve were finally in their car, alone, headed for their honeymoon, the beginning of a long life together.

Chapter 29

Now that the wedding was over and Leslie and Steve were on their honeymoon, Mona turned her mind and efforts to getting ready for Christmas. Bob brought home the Christmas tree and together they decorated it, remembering in years past how Jacob and Leslie had loved to hang their own special ornaments on the tree, and they had always made sure their Christmas stockings were hung well in sight of that jolly old man. They reminisced as they added the lights and laughed a little at how Jake ripped open his packages and how Leslie had carefully saved the bows on hers. They had a lot to be thankful for. Jake in college, Leslie now married, and one of these years, hopefully, grandchildren. In a gush of emotion, Mona thought of Angel. Not the little dead baby, but a six-year-old sitting up in a hospital bed. In her own heart she believed that child was indeed Angel. She wanted to tell Bob, but he would surely think she had lost her mind. But then he didn't see her—she did. Mona rationalized that if this child was truly Angel, how many lives would be torn apart? If it was not, what a turmoil it would cause. She sighed and knew this was something she had to forget. Forget? Well, at least she had to lay it to rest, but she would never forget. She still planned to find out where the Lamberts lived so she could at least see the child again. All of the family would be home for Christmas, and Mona had invited Steve's parents as well. They would all be eager to hear about the honeymoon. Mona and Bob had never been to Hawaii, but they were very pleased to have had a hand in sending the "kids" there for their honeymoon.

Leslie and Steve were indeed enjoying the warm weather and the marvelous love songs of Hawaii. They did all the tourist things. They visited the Dole pineapple factory, visited Hilo Hattie's, where they bought muumuus for Mona and Norma, and then took a trip to the *Arizona* Memorial. It was a solemn and touching occasion when they stood on the memorial reading the names of those who perished and looked down into the water at the USS *Arizona* still resting there. They went to a luau and witnessed this great Hawaiian tradition and enjoyed the wonderful fun and entertainment there. They did a lot of sightseeing, but the real joy came from just being together.

They strolled the beach early in the morning, watching the birds and seeing the slow-moving surf. Later in the day when the swells began to pound the shore, they watched surfers riding the big ones. Neither of them wanted to try that kind of surfing, but it was beautiful to watch. In the evenings, they went to dinner and watched the beautiful hula girls performing the lovely dances of the islands. Later, they made love in their room, listening to the ocean and still hearing the music from afar. Here, away from the world, they made their own music and pledged again and again to love each other forever. It was a perfect time.

Joan and Paul had been planning for Christmas, also. This year they wanted to include Hannah and Tonya. When Joan asked Hannah, tears came into her eyes and she said, "Oh, Joan, that is so thoughtful of you. Tonya and I put up a small tree, but I expect we would have been pretty lonely—just the two of us." The girls, of course, were delighted. Mary Ann and Tonya had been spending a lot of time together, and both Joan and Hannah had been afraid it would put a strain on their relationship, but apparently it had just brought them closer together. Mary Ann still said Tonya saved her life by getting help so quickly when she hurt her arm. Sometimes Tonya and Mary Ann would look carefully at the scar to see if it was going away. If it didn't, Mary Ann knew she could have it fixed. The doctor had told her. She tried not to think about it, but she saw other people looking at it, and it made her feel funny. She wore long sleeves a lot and that hid the ragged scar.

Joan asked Hannah what she thought about asking Peter for Christmas, also. Hannah really liked Peter. He was a great boss, but she blushed a little as she said, "Joan, I get the feeling you are trying a little matchmaking. Of course, invite Peter if you want to, but he doesn't have any designs on me outside of work. We have become good friends." Joan didn't voice her thoughts, but she had seen Peter watching Hannah when she didn't know it, and what she saw in his eyes was much more than a passing interest in his secretary.

Joan and Hannah had promised the girls to take them to the mall one afternoon to do some last-minute shopping and to see Santa Claus. They loved to see the jolly man, but both giggled as they stood back and watched the little kids sit on his lap, have their picture made, and leave with him their list for toys for

126

Christmas. Mary Ann and Tonya were too grown up for sitting on his lap, but they had their pictures made, one on each side of Santa. They loved looking in the windows and picking out things they would like. Tonya liked the pretty clothes; Mary Ann liked the lifelike baby dolls. She liked to dress them and play like she was the mother looking out for her baby. She seemed to remember her mom bathing her, rocking her, and always taking such good care of her.

Mona had gone to Warren to see Jacob, and they both needed to go to the mall to pick up some last-minute gifts. There was a big crowd, so they separated to meet later in front of the nut stand. Shopping would be faster this way. As Mona hurried along she saw the children gathered in front of Santa. Leslie had always liked seeing Santa. As she looked, she saw two little girls having their pictures made. She looked at the smiling little dark-haired girl and then glanced at the other one. Her heart pounded, she was short of breath, and she felt as if she would faint. There she was, the same little girl from the hospital—Leslie all over again. She looked around and yes, there was Mrs. Lambert with another lady, obviously the other little girl's mother. Mona watched as the two girls talked to their mothers and hand in hand went off into the mall. Thoughts of shopping or anything else went out of Mona's head except this vision of Leslie eighteen years ago. There was no doubt whatsoever in her mind that this child was her grandchild—the one she thought they buried. Dr. Williams had thought she was crazy. If she told Bob or anyone else, they, too, would think she had lost her marbles. She certainly couldn't talk to Leslie about it. Here she was just on her honeymoon, and Steve knew nothing of Angel. Maybe she was just being foolish. Maybe everyone has a look-alike and this was Leslie's, but then the odd coincidences came flooding back to haunt her. Born the same day, same hospital, same doctor, same nurse, that in her mind she could still see changing places with the babies' cribs. She was still off somewhere in a daze when Jacob touched her arm and asked, "All through, Mom?" She had no desire to look further, so she said, "Yes, I didn't find what I wanted so I'll have to look later." They left the mall. She dropped Jake off, and then she started the thirty-mile drive to Evanston. All the way home she tried to clear her head. She had to forget this foolishness. Years ago Angel was laid to rest, and she, Bob, and Leslie had agreed to let her rest in peace. The past is past, she kept telling herself. Leave it alone.

Chapter 30

Christmas passed and New Year's, and everyone seemed to get back in the normal swing of things. Leslie and Steve finally found a house for rent with a lovely fenced back yard, for children to play someday, until they could find a nice house they could afford to buy. Steve's office was doing very well, and Leslie was back at the hospital. Leslie was still walking on clouds. She had never in her life felt so wonderful as she did with Steve. It seemed that they each knew what the other was thinking even before they spoke. Dr. Chris told Leslie she never looked better, and the perpetual glow seemed to spread all around.

The holidays at Joan's all turned out very well. In spite of Hannah's denial of anything except friendly affection between her and Peter, Joan was delighted to see how attentive Peter was to Hannah and to Tonya. One day something real good could come of this relationship. Paul teased her about being a matchmaker, but he was secretly pleased.

After the rush and excitement of the holidays Mona felt a letdown. Not exactly depression, but a loneliness. Jacob was back at school, and Leslie and Steve were in a home of their own. Bob was having to be out of town more lately, and Mona was restless. She still worked three days a week, and she still spent some volunteer time at the hospital, but something was wrong in her life. She couldn't define it. She just knew she felt lonely and depressed even when Bob was home. Here she was forty-seven years old. Maybe that was the reason. She tried to give herself pep talks and it all sounded good, but at the end, she felt the same. She hadn't told anyone the way she was feeling. Bob would think she was nuts, and she certainly didn't want to say anything to Leslie. She'd considered talking to Norma, she was a good friend, but it all sounded so silly.

One afternoon the phone rang, and a woman's voice asked for Bob. Mona explained that Bob was out of town and wouldn't arrive home until around six o'clock. She asked her name and if she'd like to leave a message. The woman said, "Oh, just tell him Sybil called. He'll know." With that she hung up. Mona thought it was a strange call, but Bob dealt with all kinds of people. She made a note to tell Bob and promptly put it out of her mind. Bob had been gone a couple of days this time, and she wanted to have dinner ready for him when he got home. Maybe she could talk to Bob and tell him about the "Angel" she saw. That might be part of the problem she was having. Bob had always been so easy to talk to, and although sometimes he strongly disagreed with her, he was always a good sounding board. She had been so lucky to have had Bob in her life all these years. She had noticed that Bob looked a little tired lately and sometimes preoccupied, but then the wedding along with Christmas and New Year's made things a little hectic for everyone.

Mona had a thick beef stew simmering when she heard the door open and Bob's voice saying, "I'm home." It was in fact a little earlier than she had expected, and it lifted her spirits somewhat. Bob hung his coat in the closet, and as they met in the living room, he put his arms around Mona and sniffed the good smells coming from the kitchen. "Just a beef stew," Mona told him.

They both sat on the sofa, and Bob stretched out his legs. With a contented sigh he held Mona's hand and said, "Boy, I'm glad to be home."

Mona snuggled up to him and said, "Me too, I'm really glad you're here. It gets mighty lonesome when you're gone." Mona glanced toward the phone, and there was the message she'd taken for Bob. "Oh," she said, "a woman called you. No message. Just that her name was Sybil and that you'd know. Some old girlfriend I should know about?" She gave him a coy look and saw him close his eyes and turn pale as a ghost.

He took a few seconds, drew a deep breath, took her hand, and said, "Yes, Mona. She is someone you should know about." Mona was in a state of shock as Bob continued. "I met Sybil about six months ago on one of my trips. I ran into her a couple of times where I ate. I was lonesome, we talked, and one thing led to another. Then one night she went back to the motel with me. I was infatuated with her, so I saw her every time I was in Porterville. She'd come discretely to my motel and leave very early in the mornings. I told her before Christmas that I could not go on that way. I loved you, and I couldn't ever see her again. She threatened then to call you. I just never thought she would. In any case I had made up my mind to tell you the truth as soon as I got home. I've been trying to get up the courage to tell you since then. I can't explain what happened to me. I don't know how I could have been so stupid. I love you and our home and our life together more than anything, and I realize I may have lost it all. I can only pray you can forgive me."

Mona sat in a daze, totally disbelieving the words she was hearing. Not her Bob with some floozy. They had it all. All the things that ever mattered in life, and it was all a lie. The rage building inside her was like the eye of a hurricane, twisting and turning and destroying everything and everyone in its path. She got up, walked to the kitchen, turned off the stew, and went to her bedroom. She sat down on the bed, the bed she and Bob had shared all these years. She was too stunned and angry to cry. It was as if she were suspended somewhere in time and had no place to go. Her life was over, nothing would ever be the same again. She had been betrayed by the one person she trusted above all. Bob came into the room pleading with her to forgive him and talk to him, but she couldn't. He was a stranger, someone she didn't know at all. She wanted to cry, to scream at him, to hurt him as he had hurt her, but she was too numb. She lay down on the bed and closed her eyes, but she couldn't shut out the total devastation she felt. Later on she got up and went back to the kitchen. She fixed herself a bowl of stew, and when she heard Bob in the living room she asked him if he would like some. He came to the kitchen. They sat at the same table and ate in silence.

Bob finally said, "Mona, please talk to me. I love you. I know I was a fool, but please don't shut me out."

Mona simply said, "I can't talk to you now. I feel as if my life has been destroyed. When I have put the pieces back together, then we'll talk." She straightened the kitchen and then went back to her room. She couldn't go to sleep. The awful words "She came to my motel" kept running through her mind, and tears began running down her cheeks. The tears came like a flood, and as sobs racked her body, she finally drifted off to sleep.

Bob paced the floor and prayed that Mona would forgive him. Maybe he shouldn't have told her the truth. His conscience had been bothering him, and he felt he had to tell her everything. He knew how hurt she would be, and he expected angry accusations, but this frozen silence he wasn't prepare for. He prayed, "Oh, God, don't let her leave me. I'm nothing without her." Why wasn't he remembering Mona when he took Sybil to his motel? He couldn't make sense of what he had done. What was he trying to prove? Had this little affair cost him his marriage and his family? My God, what would Leslie and Jacob think of their father now? He put his head down and sobbed—the despair of a broken man.

Chapter 31

Mary Ann thought this Christmas was the best one she had ever had. She hadn't really wished for anything special for Christmas. She still loved stuffed animals and books and pretty clothes. What made it so special was sharing it with Tonya. Mary Ann sometimes wished she had a sister or even a brother, and her mama had explained to her that sometimes God made it possible to have only one special child. Now that she had Tonya, she no longer wished for anyone else. Since that mean old Ralph was gone, she and Tonya could spend more and more time together. Even Hannah was more fun to be around. She was prettier, too. She'd had her hair cut and smiled ever so much more. Mary Ann felt sorry for Tonya not having a real father like her papa, and sometimes Tonya told her things about her father. Tonya didn't really remember him, but Hannah had told her what a nice, loving man he was.

Mary Ann's arm bothered her some—mostly the way it looked. The skin was sort of puckered and sunk in all along where the cut was. She tried not to notice, but it made her feel bad when people stared at it or mentioned it. Her mama kept telling her to be patient, and it would look better. When she got older, she could have it fixed. Tonya told her it was her mark of bravery because she thought Mary Ann had been very brave when it happened. But Mary Ann didn't think she had been very brave. In fact, she had been very scared. Dr. Chris had been nice and made her feel safe.

Mary Ann wanted to take gymnastics lessons and Papa had agreed, but she really wanted Tonya to, also. Tonya wasn't sure yet whether or not her mom could afford classes right now. Mr. Magness had given her a raise just before Christmas, so maybe they could both go to gymnastics classes soon. Mary Ann really didn't want to go without Tonya.

Joan had noticed a change in Mary Ann in the last month or so. She seemed so grown up. When she mentioned it to Paul, he just reminded her that their baby was growing up and in such a lovely way. They both thanked God over and over for allowing them to have such a remarkable child. If they could have chosen a little girl, they would have wanted one just like Mary Ann. When they remembered how close they came to losing her when she was born, it still scared them. They could still see that tiny little doll, so small and so fragile lying in the hospital crib. A far cry from the healthy little girl she was today. They knew that all parents probably felt the same way, but Mary Ann was smart, too. She was sensitive and loving, and it wasn't easy to fool her. She seemed to have a sixth sense about everything, and she always felt what was going on around her. It was noticeable how Mary Ann thought about Tonya's needs and how Tonya protected Mary Ann. They couldn't have been closer if they had been sisters. Joan thought of Peter and Hannah and wondered if they would finally get together. Peter would be good for Tonya, too. Paul accused her of trying to be a matchmaker. She really wasn't, although she certainly thought they would be a perfect pair. She had begun to think of Hannah as a very close friend. She had been so quiet in the beginning, but now that she and Ralph were divorced, and he was out of her life, she had blossomed. She was a bright, intelligent woman, and working for Peter had brought out her best qualities. It was hard to imagine how being married to someone like Ralph could so completely stifle her personality. Joan loved just to sit at Hannah's, in the cozy kitchen, over a cup of coffee while Hannah told her the news of the day. Theirs had become an easy-going relationship. With Tonya and Mary Ann so close, it was just a natural. Paul enjoyed Hannah's company, too, and often thought what a fool Ralph had been to give up two such wonderful people as Hannah and Tonya. It would be nice if Hannah found someone worthy of sharing their lives.

Peter mulled over the events through Christmas and smiled contentedly to himself as he remembered the happy festivities at the Lamberts'. It was the first Christmas in a long time that he had really felt at home and comfortable among friends. He, Joan, and Paul had known each other a long time, but he suspected that the presence of Hannah was what made him feel so happy. Since she had been in his office, it was a real pleasure to go to work. She was so organized. She seemed to sense his moods and knew just when he needed to talk, and she kept his clients happy. In fact, there wasn't anything he didn't like about Hannah. It was certainly his lucky day when Joan brought Hannah to his office. His outlook on life was brighter, and who knew what the new year could bring.

134

Tonya had had a marvelous Christmas. The best one she ever had, she thought. It wasn't just the presents. It was being with Mary Ann and seeing her mother so happy. Everyone laughed a lot, and she didn't have to be afraid she would make old Ralph mad. She could just be herself, and she didn't have to stay in her room all alone. She and Mary Ann sat at the dinner table with the grown ups, and everyone was so nice to her— especially Peter. She thought he kind of liked her mother, and he seemed to like her, too. He had even given her mother a raise in pay, so maybe now she could go to gymnastics classes with Mary Ann. Mary Ann had said she didn't want to go without her. Tonya was a little scared of all that running and tumbling, but if Mary Ann wanted to, then she would, too. Maybe it wasn't as hard as it looked. Things were going to be a lot better for her and her mom in the new year. She could already tell that. Boy, getting rid of old Ralph made everything better. She didn't have to feel afraid all the time anymore. She could even make herself a peanut-butter sandwich after school. It didn't spoil her supper, either.

Chapter 32

Weeks had gone by since that fateful call from Sybil, and Mona still hadn't been able to think straight. She and Bob shared the same house. They ate together and still slept in the same bed, being careful not to touch each other. They spoke civilly to one another, and when Leslie or Jacob was around, they seemed the same, but Mona was beginning to wonder if anything would ever be the same again.

She had told Bob that when she could and when she had things all worked out in her mind, they would talk. She had tried to figure out what she had done wrong to cause Bob to go to bed with some other woman. She thought that she had been a good wife. Their sex life, she believed, was wonderful. Granted, they didn't go at it every night like they did when they were younger, but she hadn't expected after twenty-six years of marriage that things would be the same. They had shared so much living together that she couldn't even imagine life without Bob. He had been her knight in shining armor, her port in a storm. She could always count on him, or so she thought. Maybe all her married life had been a lie. She had to try to put into perspective all that had happened. Simply put, Bob had had an affair. He wasn't in love with the other woman. He didn't want a divorce, quite the opposite. He had begged Mona not to leave him. In fact, she believed him when he said he didn't know what got into him. The hurt still made her skin crawl, and the thoughts of Bob doing all those intimate things with another woman made her sick to her stomach. Sybil hadn't called the house again, and Mona felt sure that Bob hadn't seen her again. She didn't know if he had spoken to her or not. Tonight when Bob came home, they had to talk. Things couldn't go on this way. It was too much strain on both of them. The simple truth was, she loved Bob and he had hurt her terribly. It would take a long time to rebuild the trust and things would never be the same, but they could have a lot of good years ahead of them. She was ready to try.

Bob had been only half alive since Sybil's phone call and his confession to Mona. Maybe he should have lied and somehow gotten out of it, but that wasn't his way. He had to take responsibility for what he had done. What made him do this, he truly didn't know. Mona was far prettier than Sybil. She certainly was smarter, and Mona had always been a good wife and mother. He had never felt anything lacking in his marriage. In fact, he often thought he was the luckiest man in the whole world. It seemed he had always been in love with Mona. She had never disappointed him. Oh sure, they quarreled sometimes, and they didn't always see things the same way, but they had never had a serious argument. He respected Mona's judgment, and she had respected his. Never in a million years would he have thought it possible for either of them to be unfaithful to the other one, and yet here he was, guilty of having an affair. How stupid could he be? Looking back, he was thoroughly embarrassed by the shoddiness of the whole thing. The sneaking around at the hotel, making sure no one saw Sybil arriving or leaving. It was all like some dimestore novel, and yet this was what he had done to Mona. He couldn't blame her if she kicked him out. He could certainly understand that her trust was gone. If he could do this to her, what else could he do?

All the way home Bob knew that he and Mona had to talk. They couldn't continue as if nothing had happened. She might kick him out, but the time had come for them to work out some kind of solution. He couldn't bear to think what might happen. He could only pray that she could forgive him.

Mona heard Bob's car pull into the driveway and quickly glanced in the hall mirror to check her hair. She wanted to look her best because this was one of the most important days in their lives. The only redeeming factor was that no one else knew of Bob's infidelity. She didn't have to see knowing looks from her friends or family. She had to swallow her pride and her hurt and try to regain all the love and trust and hope that she and Bob had always had. When Bob came in, she met him in the entryway, put her arms around him, and hugged him close. He kissed her, and it seemed that nothing had ever happened.

He said, "I have missed you so, being near you, but unable to touch you or love you."

Mona, eyes teary, said, "Bob, I love you. You are the same man I married. You made a mistake, a very big one. One that almost destroyed our home, but I can't let that happen. If I'd made the same mistake, could you have forgiven me? We'll never know the answer to that one, but I do know that I want us to try to put all of this behind us and be again the happy couple we've always been. Can you do this?"

Bob couldn't believe his ears. Mona was offering him another chance. Oh, thank you, God! "Mona, I promise you that I will do my best to be the kind of husband you deserve. I love you. I've never stopped loving you, and I will spend the rest of my life trying to make this up to you. I can't expect you to forget it overnight, and I am so sorry and ashamed to have put you through this. I can't even give you a good explanation as to why it happened. Just try to believe me when I tell you something like this will never happen again." They hugged and kissed again, and arm in arm they went upstairs for Bob to change out of his business clothes. Mona could smell the meatloaf in the oven, but it wasn't food they had on their minds just now. Supper could wait.

Chapter 33

Leslie had never been so happy in all her life. Living with Steve was wonderful. The first few months had been hectic, each getting use to the other's schedules, but now everything just fell into place. They had been looking for a house to possibly buy if they could afford such a thing. They were very lucky to find the house they wanted. They had been driving around looking desperately for someplace, just as the owner was placing a "for sale" sign in the yard. Just moments before, they had been admiring this very same house. It was white with green shutters and a porch on the front with white railings all around. The back yard had a steel fence—a perfect place for a dog or, she said as she nudged Steve, children. He laughed as he said, "You could start with one child."

"Maybe we'll have twins or triplets," she countered.

The grass was lush and well cared for, and the flowerbeds around the front and down the walkway were well groomed. Someone loved this house. They didn't know if they could buy a house right now or not, but they wanted to look at this one. Leslie was impressed as they went inside. The living room and dining room were bright and cheery. It felt like a comfortable home. The owners kept showing them around, and Leslie and Steve both fell in love with everything. There were three bedrooms, two bathrooms, and a nice laundry room. The kitchen had beautiful cabinets, and everything was spotless. The couple was leaving and moving to another climate for the woman's health. She told Leslie she really hated leaving this house, she loved it so.

As they left, Steve told them that he and Leslie were really interested in the house, but it might take a few days for him to know if the money was available. They assured them that they would have first chance at the house. All the way home Leslie kept asking Steve, "Do you really like that house? And do you think we can get a loan? I loved the house, but if it doesn't work out, something else will." Leslie had already learned in life that you don't always get things just the way you want, but how could she complain when she married someone so marvelous as Steve? There were still a few dark shadows hovering around. A dark secret that only on rare occasions came to light, but she quickly brushed them away, reveling instead in her complete happiness with Steve.

Leslie wanted to call Mona and tell her about the house, but she was afraid she might jinx the deal if she got too excited too soon. Steve was going to check on the financing today, and she realized that it wasn't that easy for a young couple to get a home loan these days. They both had a good income, but you never know about bankers.

Leslie kept seeing the house over and over in her mind. The window dressings would all stay, the woman had told her, so that was one thing she'd not have to worry about at first. She and Steve each had some furniture, so they could reasonably furnish the house. She kept seeing her sofa in the living room and their big bed in the master bedroom. One of these days they wanted children, but they had time to get a baby's room ready.

Leslie's life had never felt so good and so safe as it had since her marriage. Dr. Chris kept teasing her and said even her work was better. She doubted that as she still took care of very sick people the best she could. She felt so sad sometimes when her efforts just were not enough.

She knew Steve would check out all possibilities. He loved the house as much as she did, and anyway, he would do anything to please Leslie. Never had he been so happy and felt so complete as he had since his marriage. There was just no one in the world quite as wonderful as Leslie.

Steve had made an appointment with Mr. Hamilton at the bank, and he was anxious to find out if they would approve his loan. Steve felt he was financially secure enough, and his family had known Mr. Hamilton for a long time. In a small town that seemed to be most important. He was a little nervous when he arrived at the bank, but he was right on time. Mr. Hamilton was expecting him. After some small talk they got right down to business. Mr. Hamilton explained to Steve that they had inspected the house, and it was well worth the money. The main problem was that Steve and Leslie had no credit established. They were young and had never bought any big items on credit. Steve hadn't had to finance his car because his wrecked car that was demolished had insurance, which paid for most of his new car, and he had paid the balance. His heart sank. He had so wanted to get this house for Leslie. He knew they could pay for it. They had the down payment in their savings, but now he had to convince Mr. Hamilton. He again explained their financial situation, and Mr. Hamilton said nothing. Finally, he said, "Steve, I believe in giving young folks a helping hand. I've known your family for years, so I feel safe in approving your loan. Just come in tomorrow with your wife to sign the papers, and the house is yours. By the way, congratulations on your wedding to such a lovely young lady. My wife was in the hospital some months ago, and Leslie took care of her. My wife was very impressed with her and probably would have had my hide if I had rejected your loan."

As soon as Steve could, he called Leslie at the hospital. He couldn't wait to tell her that the house was theirs. Their first real home together. This was a day to remember. They could have the house in thirty days. Already he was planning on enlisting Jacob and Jack to help with the moving, and he suspected that Bob and his dad would be there, too.

Leslie was so excited when Steve gave her the good news. Everything seemed just about perfect. She wanted to tell Mona right away. Her mom had always been supportive of her. She didn't know what she would do without her. Mona had seemed a little distant lately. Surely she wasn't sick. She had tried to look cheery, but Leslie could tell something was amiss. Tonight they would call Mona and Bob and Steve's folks. She knew Jacob would be pleased, too. In fact, the last time she had seen Jake, he had been quite excited. One of these days soon he would finish school, and she had a feeling that Emily had a lot to do with it. Jake had seemed more and more enchanted with her. Leslie smiled to herself. Yes, she knew what it was to be in love.

Chapter 34

Mona was thinking of her two grandchildren as she made an apple pie. She had already made sugar cookies. This was what Cynthia liked, and she always included her baby brother, Patrick. In fact, he loved anything that Cynthia gave him. She was the little mother.

It didn't seem possible that it had been four years since Steve had called to tell her Leslie had gone into labor and she had rushed to the hospital. It was rough for a while, and they had all worried. Leslie had been in hard labor for a long time, and it didn't look good. Dr. Chris was ready to do a Caesarean, but Leslie protested and pleaded, "Dr. Chris, I can do it." And she did—a beautiful baby girl, six and a half pounds, nineteen inches long. A plump little bundle of joy. Steve had stayed with her the whole time, and when he came out of delivery, tears of gratitude and joy ran down his face. "Leslie was so brave," he said. He had been so afraid when Leslie had tried too hard and the baby wouldn't come. They had already picked the name Cynthia Ann. She was a little beauty. Her hair was dark like his, and of course you couldn't tell about her eyes. He hoped they would be blue like Leslie's, but he was secretly pleased that Leslie thought she looked like him. He suspected that Dr. Chris would keep Leslie longer in the hospital than normal because she had really had a bad time. Even he could tell how weak she was, although she tried to reassure him that everything was fine.

And then there was Patrick, born two years later with no problem at all. He was his mother's boy. No doubt about it. He had blond hair and deep sea-blue eyes. Cynthia's eyes were brown like Steve's, and her disposition was all Steve's. She was the little mother for Patrick, and he doted on everything she did. Mona felt so good about both of them. She and Bob loved being grandparents. These babies seemed to wipe all the past problems away. Once in a while Mona thought of Angel, but with these two babies in her life she swiftly tried to put her feelings away. Only one other time had she seen Mary Ann Lambert. She had read in the newspaper that a gymnastics meet was being held in Warren and that Mary Ann and another girl, Tonya something or other, were among the top contenders. She had driven over to the school and watched the team march in. There she was, Leslie all over again. Mona hadn't stayed long. The strain was too much. Every move Mary Ann made was Leslie's move. Mona's heart was pounding and again, as six years ago, she knew that this young lady was Angel. It hadn't been easy to walk away, but she knew she had to. Leslie and Steve were so happy with their family. How could she dredge up the past that might well destroy them all? Since then she vowed never to try to see Mary Ann again, just to be happy with Cynthia and Patrick. Anyway, she'd be a grandmother again in a few months. Jacob had finally married his Emily, and they were expecting. They also lived in Warren, so all of the family was very close.

Leslie was back to work at the hospital now. She had taken a leave of absence when Patrick was born. She wanted to be home with him and Cynthia for a while. She had a wonderful woman who came every day to take care of the children and the house. Her name was Martha Cabot, and she was a real jewel. She was in her early fifties, widowed, and living a long way from her own grandchildren. She was extremely happy to work for Leslie and Steve, and she loved the children. Leslie was sometimes jealous when Cynthia would tell her all the things Miss Martha did for her and Patrick. Leslie had missed her work, and with Miss Martha there, she felt perfectly content to go back. Nursing had been a big part of her life, and she had missed it. Dr. Williams had finally retired, and Dr. Chris was busier than ever. He was particularly pleased when Leslie came back. He had missed her, too, although he had been very understanding about her family's needs.

Mona had given up her three-day-a-week job at the dental clinic. She still did volunteer work at the hospital, but she was always ready to go with Bob and to spend time with Cynthia and Patrick. Bob didn't have to go out of town as much anymore, and this gave them more time to be together. It seemed that they had actually grown closer together the last few years. After the near tragedy of six years ago, they both were well aware of how close they had come to losing each other. Of course, Mona could never forget the devastating feeling of betrayal, but she didn't dwell on it, and she had long ago accepted the fact that anyone could make a mistake. She couldn't imagine her life without Bob, and she knew he felt the same way about her.

Leslie couldn't imagine her life any more perfect than it was. Life with Steve had been everything she had hoped for, and with Cynthia and Patrick, she felt especially blessed. They had been in their house for six years now, and she loved it more every day. It was the perfect house in which to raise children. She could watch the children playing in the back yard, often times joining in their games. Patrick tried so hard to keep up with his big sister. She thought Cynthia was a beautiful little daddy's girl. She was more and more like Steve every day. Dark-brown hair glistening in the sun, and those big, brown, questioning eyes always wanting to know everything. When Leslie came home from work, Cynthia would tell her everything she and Patrick and Miss Martha had done all day. Then Cynthia would want to hear what Leslie had done. Of course, when Steve came home, it started all over again. Patrick lay his head on Leslie's lap, but kept his eyes on Cynthia. He mimicked everything she did. They certainly didn't look alike. Patrick had Leslie's big blue eyes and golden hair. Even his smile and his baby moves all were like Leslie. She patted his head and smelled the baby smell of him as she silently thanked God for these two babies. Just looking at them filled her heart to overflowing. How could she have been so lucky? She sometimes imagined Angel, twelve years old, helping with her brother and sister. She tried to erase the image from her mind and wondered if the day would ever come when she could put Angel out of her mind forever. Remembering did no one any good.

After graduating from college, Jacob and Steve opened their own public accountant offices. At first it had been a little scary, but after about a year, they picked up some very good accounts, and now they were doing very well—so well that they had expanded their offices and hired four new employees. Jake and Steve worked well together, and now that Jake and Emily were expecting their first child, they had more in common. They had been married three years, and they had wanted to start their family while they were still young. Emily had been Jacob's only serious girlfriend. Her father was the sheriff of their town and had given Jacob a hard time at first. Emily always said lovingly that her dad's badge kept the boys at bay.

Actually, Emily's dad had liked Jake right from the start and wasn't at all displeased when he asked for Emily's hand. He, too, was anxiously awaiting his grandchild. The latest word was that it was probably a boy. Secretly, Jake was hoping for a son.

Chapter 35

Mary Ann was excited and very nervous when she knew she had been selected to represent her school in the gymnastics meet for the junior high. Tonya had also been selected, and they were both delighted. Tonya was confident that Mary Ann would win everything. Tonya was especially good on the floor exercise. She was well muscled and strong for this event, but Mary Ann's dainty figure made her perfect for the balance beam, the vault, and the bars.

Mary Ann and Tonya had both started in gymnastics when they were six, and both of them had worked very hard to excel. It had been difficult for Hannah at first to be able to allow Tonya to take lessons, but Peter had been generous and she got a raise just in time for Tonya to begin classes with Mary Ann. Right from the start they had been strong competitors, one time Mary Ann ahead, the next time Tonya. They always rooted for the other one in competition.

Hannah and Peter had finally gotten married three years ago, and they had moved into a new house that Peter had built for them. One thing he had insisted on was that he be allowed to adopt Tonya. He told her he wanted to be sure that she would always be his. Hannah was touched by this, and Tonya was delighted. Now they were forever free of Ralph. Tonya had used his name in school, but now she had a daddy like Mary Ann's papa. Tonya Magness! She said it over and over, and for the first time in her young life, she could relate to a real family. Peter doted on Tonya, and Hannah laughingly accused him of wanting Tonya and that was why he married her. Things had never gone so right for them. Peter had been a bachelor for a long time. In fact, he never expected to marry. After being jilted so long ago, he didn't have a lot of trust in women. He had longed for a home and family, but the right person hadn't come along until he met Hannah. At first he felt sympathetic toward her, and later after she was working in his office, he began to see all the good things she did. She was kind and gentle, but she also was made of steel. She was the kind of person you could always depend on. Life had not treated her kindly, but you never heard her complain. She had her Tonya, and she would never be defeated. Peter was drawn more and more to

Hannah, and he began to think of her as more than just a friend. He didn't know how she felt, and he didn't want to spoil a good friendship, so he kept quiet. Actually it was Joan who finally recognized what he felt for Hannah and advised him to start taking her out. Hannah had admired Peter from the beginning, and when he asked her out, she was pleased and began to feel alive again. The years with Ralph left a bitter taste, but she knew that there was more to life than just working and going home each day alone to be with Tonya. Finally when Peter admitted he loved her, she knew that she loved him, too. When they planned the wedding, Tonya was delighted. They had a simple ceremony in a local chapel with Joan and Paul and Mary Ann and Tonya attending. Tonya stayed with Mary Ann while the happy couple took a short honeymoon to Myrtle Beach. Hannah had never been anywhere before, and she vowed that they would come back again to bring Tonya. Peter was having a house built before he proposed, and with a few minor changes the house was soon ready for the three of them.

When the day of the gymnastics meet finally came, Hannah took the day off, and Peter closed the office early so he'd be there in time to see Tonya perform. Joan and Paul would also be there. The mothers were almost as nervous as Tonya and Mary Ann, each wanting their child to win, but not wanting the other one to lose. Joan had simply told Mary Ann just to do her best and that was the only important thing. Winning would be nice, but it wasn't everything. Hannah had told Tonya that she and Peter were proud of her and that no matter the scores, she would always be a winner to them.

Tonya and Mary Ann didn't say too much to each other except "do your best; don't worry about me." They hugged just before they marched out and vowed to be the best two there. As the girls saluted and all came marching out, heads held high, an awed hush came over the spectators. It was a touching sight, and everyone was bursting with pride. If the girls had been nervous, you couldn't tell it now.

There were four teams, each with eight girls. The gymnasium was divided into four different sections, with events in each of the four categories being held simultaneously. Mary Ann's team would start with the bars and end with the floor exercise. Both girls knew who the strongest competition would be. Reputations travel fast among the area schools, and they also knew that the two of them were considered the best on their team. That was a lot of responsibility—to know others were depending on you. Of course, individually, it was an honor, but a good performance by Tonya and Mary Ann also helped the team's chances of winning the overall competition.

Mary Ann drew number one on the bars and Tonya number four. Mary Ann never liked to be first, but she saluted the judges and stepped quickly into position to be helped up to reach the bars. Once there, all her concentration was on her routine.

Joan could hardly breathe as she watched that slim figure swing and turn from one bar to the other. This was the first time she had seen Mary Ann perform in competition. When Mary Ann did a flip into her dismount, Joan began to breathe normally again. Mary Ann's feet had been a little apart, but she landed solidly. It was a good exercise.

When Tonya's turn came, Hannah clutched Peter's hand and almost wanted to close her eyes. Her palms were sweaty, and she couldn't help thinking, what if she falls? Tonya went right into her routine, and it looked good. She had just a little back step on landing, but she was pleased. Mary Ann was there to give her a hug and to congratulate her when she finished. Both girls had fair scores, Mary Ann slightly ahead. There was still a lot of competition and a long way to go.

Joan and Hannah weren't sure their nerves could stand too much of this, but as they watched the other teams perform, they began to really believe their girls were better. Tonya scored higher on the vault than Mary Ann, but Mary Ann did better on the balance beam. Actually, they were very close. Two girls from the opposing teams were keeping close, also. Any team could win, and the individual overall was up for grabs. Tonya was first in her floor exercise, and this was generally her strong event. She ran and tumbled and danced to her music and was a delight to watch. Watching from the sidelines, Mary Ann felt that no one would beat Tonya on the floor. As she made her last tumbling run and ended with her music in a split, the audience applauded and cheered. Hannah and Peter were bursting with pride.

When it finally came Mary Ann's turn and her music

started, a hush came over the crowd. Her music was different, and she was like a forest nymph, turning and twisting and seeming to fly. She was like a fairy, beautiful to watch. Mary Ann didn't seem to have the muscles and strength of Tonya, but it was as if she didn't need it and that it was effortless to accomplish all the requirements of her routine. As she fell to her knees and bowed her head at the finish, she, too, received cheers and applause. Tonya was waiting to hug her and said, "Mary Ann, that was the best you have ever done!" No matter what the final score, both girls were very pleased with themselves. Their coach was proud of her girls and had them all in a huddle around her. To her, they were all winners. Mary Ann was higher on the beam, Tonya on the vault. Another girl from another team was higher on the bars. The floor exercise would decide the overall champion. When the judges finally posted the scores, Tonya was a fraction of a point ahead. As Mary Ann congratulated her, Tonya said, "Oh, Mary Ann, you were perfect. You should have won." But Mary Ann was sincerely happy for her friend, her very best friend, the one who had saved her life six years ago. She even promised Tonya, "I'll beat you next time."

The parents were all relieved it was over, and after getting permission from the coach, they were able to take the girls with them. Joan wondered how many of these meets she could stand. The girls weren't nearly as nervous as she and Hannah had been. This was only junior-high competition. What about high school and then where? Peter and Paul shook their heads. They wondered, too, if the women could stand much more. The girls felt okay. It was the mothers who fell apart.

By the time they all reached the pizza place, the day's events were forgotten. They were just hungry. It was at this event that Mona saw her Angel again.

152

Chapter 36

Hannah couldn't remember ever being so happy and content as she had the last few years. After she had gone to work with Peter, she had, for the first time in her adult life, begun to feel like she was a whole person, capable of supporting herself and making a good home for Tonya. Ralph had broken her spirit and taken away all her self-esteem. She was afraid all the time and hadn't really known what a prisoner she had been. It had apparently taken the fact that Ralph was sexually abusing Tonya to open her eyes and give her the strength to get out. Tonya was her whole life, and she truly believed she didn't need anyone else—until she met Peter. She admired Peter right from the start, then later they became friends. She learned a lot about how skittish he was around women. He wasn't at all interested in a serious relationship. She also saw how kind he was to Tonya and how he watched other children with their parents. Peter was meant to be a father. As their friendship grew, so did Hannah's feelings for Peter. She had decided after Ralph that she would never be ready for love again, but gradually she began to notice the symptoms. She listened for Peter's footsteps in the morning, and she loved to see him sitting at his desk, looking out his window just watching the birds and the people hurrying around. At night she still carried the image of him home with her, and often she fantasized about what it would be like having Peter come home with her every night and about Tonya being his little girl. She knew she was being silly. Peter hadn't even asked her out for a social date. Their association was strictly business. The first real date he asked her on, she was as jittery as a schoolgirl. When she had called Joan to ask if Tonya could stay with Mary Ann, Joan had said, "Of course, and it's about time Peter asked you out!"

Peter had thought about Hannah a lot. She had made such a difference in his office life, and there were times he couldn't begin to concentrate on his work for thinking of Hannah in the outer office. He fantasized, too, about having a home and a family, and the faces that always came to mind were Hannah's and Tonya's. He knew that Hannah's life was better financially now. He saw to that, and he knew that both she and Tonya had started to bloom. Hannah was someone he could talk to, and he appreciated her friendship. He knew he was feeling much more than friendship, but he certainly didn't want to mess up what he had by putting moves on her. Maybe she wasn't ready, or maybe she didn't feel the same way about him. Joan had finally convinced him that he should ask Hannah out, so he did. After that first date, he couldn't see enough of her. Yes, he was in love with Hannah and with Tonya. He almost died of fright when he finally declared his love for her and asked her to marry him. He couldn't believe his ears as Hannah clung to him and said over and over, "I love you, Peter. I have never loved anyone as I do you."

Some months before, he had started building a house. He was tired of always living in a rented apartment. Now that he was going to have a family, he needed a different house, so he and Hannah decided on some changes that would make the house perfect for the three of them. When they told Tonya that they were going to be married, she was ecstatic. She would at last have a real home and a father all her own.

When they finally set the date for the wedding, it coincided with the completion of the house. When they came back from their short honeymoon, they came home to their new house. They had already moved their things in, and Tonya called this their honeymoon house.

Tonya was delighted when her mother and Peter told her that they wanted to get married. She was pleased they wanted her to tell them what she thought about it. Peter had explained that he loved her mother, but he also loved her and wanted to be her father. He had told her that he knew her real father would want someone to look after her, and he wanted to be the one. Tonya remembered how nice Ralph had seemed at first and then how mean he had become, and she was a little scared. She and Hannah were doing okay alone. Sure, sometimes she wished for a papa like Mary Ann's, but her papa had died. Peter talked to her for a long time, telling her that he understood how she felt and that he and Hannah could wait until she was sure about it. Of course, she talked it over with Mary Ann. Mary Ann explained that not everyone was like Ralph and that she already knew how kind Peter was and how she already liked him. Yes, Mary Ann was right, he was a good person. She went directly to the phone and called Peter's office. When Hannah answered,

Tonya asked to speak to Peter. Puzzled, Hannah buzzed Peter. When Peter answered, Tonya said, "Peter, I've decided that Mom and I will marry you. Then I'll be your girl, and you'll be my daddy." Later as Peter told Hannah, holding her in his arms, they both shared happy tears. Tonya had not been sorry they had accepted Peter's proposal. Life had never been as good as it was now. She was Tonya Magness and had been for the last nine years. She had almost forgotten the years before Peter became her father. The things she still remembered were the white lines at the bottom of her dresses.

Chapter 37

Leslie had never been more content in her life. The children, Cynthia and Patrick, were growing up, and Steve's and Jacob's business was doing very well. Her job in the hospital was never better, yet there was a little nagging feeling that things were not all that perfect. Something was not right. A few days before, she had had lunch with Mona, and later she thought her mother didn't look too well. She had seemed quiet, and Leslie thought she had lost weight. Everything had seemed good with her and Bob the last time they had been home. She couldn't quite put her finger on it, but she felt a little uneasy. Maybe she could get her mother to come in to Dr. Chris for a check-up. She had meant to look on Mona's chart and see when she had last had a good going over.

Mona hadn't said anything to Bob, but she hadn't been feeling up to par. She didn't want to worry him, and she had lost some weight. She really didn't know why. She had a good appetite. She didn't relish the idea, but if she kept feeling so down, she'd have to go for a check-up. She hadn't had a complete physical in a few years. Guess old age was creeping up on her. She hated to think that she was nearing fifty-eight. Time had gone so fast. Cynthia was ten; Patrick was eight; Michael Jacob, Jake's boy, was six. She couldn't believe how the time had just gone somewhere. Maybe part of her feelings—yes, depression—might have to do with suddenly waking up to the fact that her children no longer needed her, and in fact her grandchildren were no longer babies. In October her "Angel" would be eighteen years old. She hadn't seen her since the gymnastics meet when Angel was twelve. Not seeing her hadn't taken her out of Mona's thoughts or out of her heart. She felt so desolate sometimes, remembering the simple service at the chapel, then seeing her as a six-year-old, and then twelve. She could close her eyes and relive every moment. If she shared her findings with Bob or Leslie, maybe it would make more sense. No one would believe her, but she was more and more certain she was right. She would love to tell Dr. Chris, but after Dr. Williams's reaction and absolute denial, she couldn't risk looking like a stupid fool again. She would make an appointment for an examination, pap smear, mammogram, blood work, et cetera, but she'd keep quiet about what was really troubling her. She felt so helpless.

Even when she and Bob had gone through the trying time, when Bob had been unfaithful, she hadn't felt this depressed. She was still angry when she thought about another woman, but she had been able to accept what she could not change and had reasonably well put that episode out of her life. She and Bob had grown so much, and their marriage had taken on an even greater dimension. She knew more and more how disastrous it would have been if she had let another woman destroy her marriage. The more she thought of Angel, the more she wanted to be able to say, "You're my first grandchild," and hold her and forever put away the image of a little doll in a white dress and a baby casket. She knew this would never be possible, but thoughts of what happened eighteen years ago still haunted her. At least Bob and Leslie had been spared the anguish she knew. Perhaps even she would have been better off never to have seen Miss Morgan moving the beds, never to have seen Mary Ann Lambert those other two times. Then she would not have known that, in fact, Angel was alive. She didn't know exactly how to prove her findings, a blood test she guessed, but it didn't take a blood test for her to know. Mary Ann was really Angel, and no doubt Mary Ann's little body was the one in the small grave. She sometimes thought she'd go nuts if she didn't tell someone, but then she thought of the havoc it would cause. Steve didn't even know about Angel, and anyone who did believed she was dead. Then what about the Lamberts and the girl who had only known herself as Mary Ann? Well, she had carried this burden for twelve years, since Angel was six, and she'd have to keep this secret forever. It was best for everyone.

Mona called Leslie and asked if she would make an appointment for her to have some tests done, and she would have an examination by Dr. Chris. Leslie made the appointments and felt somewhat better knowing her mother was finally admitting that she hadn't felt too well and wanted to do something about it. What Leslie couldn't know was that the real reason for Mona's depression could not come to light.

Chapter 38

Mary Ann could hardly believe that she was a senior in high school. She was happy thinking about graduating and going on to college. She had been a part of almost all the school activities. She'd been a cheerleader, member of the Beta Club, member of the gymnastics team, editor of the yearbook, homecoming queen, and voted most likely to succeed. It had been a busy year, and she would be glad to finish, but in a way she didn't want things to change. She and Tonya were still best friends, and most of the time they dated together. She had a number of friends that were male, but no one really special. Papa had told her she had lots of time to find a special boy, and so she didn't think too much about it. Right now she was wondering how she would rank scholastically in her class. She knew she would be close to valedictorian, but the announcement hadn't been made yet. She hoped she would make it, but Tonya was in the running, too, and she didn't want her to be disappointed. It had always been this way. She and Tonya always competing and Mary Ann wanting to win, but not wanting Tonya to lose. The wins and losses had been pretty even up to now, and Tonya had always laughed and said, "Mary Ann, don't be so serious. One of us will win." And that was all that was important to Tonya. Mary Ann was like her second self. Sisters could not have been closer, and since neither one of them had siblings, they filled the bill for each other.

A few years back Mary Ann had had plastic surgery on her arm. Finally the ragged scar was gone, and her arm was as smooth as the other one. She hadn't realized how much it had bothered her until it was gone. Tonya always called it her badge of bravery, but it was a reminder to Mary Ann of the time Tonya saved her life.

Mary Ann often felt that something special must have been given to her. Her mama and papa had always been so wonderful to her. She had heard some girls complain about their parents, but Mary Ann did not complain about hers. They had advised her, discussed her problems with her, and, above all, loved her as she loved them. She couldn't imagine life without them, and that was the only cloud in her horizon. Of course, she was going to college, and she could go right here in

Warren and continue to live at home, but she really had been drawn to the school of nursing, and she would have to move away to pursue that. She had talked to Papa about it, and he had encouraged her to go after what she really wanted, even if it took her away from home. She'd thought about other professions, but it always came back to nursing. It may have started when she hurt her arm, and she saw the tender care the nurses gave her. It was as if she were compelled to help others. Tonya was just as set on following Peter's footsteps and would study to be a lawyer. That was another thing that troubled Mary Ann. She and Tonya would probably be separated, too. She could change her mind, but as Papa had said, "Follow your heart and your dreams, and everything else will all work out." Papa was so smart! No wonder he taught in college. She'd have to really make up her mind soon and apply to the college she chose, otherwise they might not have a place for her.

While Mary Ann was pondering her future, Tonya was, also. She knew without a doubt she wanted to go into law. Living with Peter for the past nine years, she had seen a lot and learned a lot about the law. Peter had allowed her to invade his office, and he had shown her so much. She admired not only him, but also the work he did that truly helped other people. She and Mary Ann actually wanted the same thing, to help people, just in different ways. It would be hard for them to be separated. They had been so close since first grade. When she looked back at her and her mom's lives before Peter, it was like it happened to someone else. The years with Ralph and the feeling of fear still troubled her sometimes. Mary Ann had been her only friend then, and nothing had changed between the two of them. Peter had changed everything for her mom and her. Not only materially, but they also knew they were loved and looked after. She could talk to Peter, and he had become the only real father she had ever known. She didn't mind too much going away to school. She knew her mom had Peter to take care of her. She thanked God every day for bringing Peter to them and making him a part of their lives. Leaving Mary Ann was another thing. All through the years they had depended on each other. She had always secretly thought Mary Ann had made her a better student. She'd had to work hard to keep up, and she had always wanted to please Mary Ann. She had secretly hoped that

Mary Ann might change her mind about nursing and go to the same college as she was, but they would keep in close touch and maybe see each other on weekends. She'd certainly miss having her around to talk to, though.

Peter and Hannah were so proud of Tonya. Everyone was waiting to see who would be valedictorian and salutatorian of their class. They knew Tonya was in the running and also Mary Ann. Those two had always competed, and Tonya had always said Mary Ann made her study harder just to keep up. Peter didn't exactly buy that. He thought Tonya was naturally smart like her mother. It did please him tremendously that Tonya wanted to be a lawyer. He already was planning for the day when she could join his law office. He loved Tonya and truly felt that she was his. He had tried to be a good father, and he was sure going to miss Tonya when she went away to school.

Joan and Paul were going through a similar time. They had tried so hard to let Mary Ann make up her own mind about college, but they could hardly bear to think of home without her. Sure, she'd visit at home, and they would visit her, but they were well aware of the fact that once a child leaves home, nothing is ever the same again. Mary Ann was likely to get an academic scholarship, and she was capable of being anything she wanted. Even from a little girl playing dolls, she had wanted to be a nurse. Joan couldn't think of anyone in her family or Paul's that had been a nurse, but Mary Ann seemed pretty determined to be one. Nursing was a great profession, a lot of hard work, but the main thing was it would take Mary Ann away to study. Joan tried to think that probably all parents felt this same way and that she and Paul were just being normal parents. They had been so grateful to have had Mary Ann that there was nothing normal about it. They just knew that they would soon be separated from their baby.

Chapter 39

When Mona told Bob she had made an appointment for a routine checkup, he felt relieved. He had thought Mona seemed a little down, and he often caught her with a strange look on her face. She didn't seem to have her usual energy, and he noticed she had lost some weight. She didn't need to lose; she had always been slim and trim. No matter how much she ate, she never seemed to put on those unwanted pounds as he did. In fact, he thought Mona's figure today was as appealing as when they had first fallen in love. That seemed like a long time ago, but then he shuddered to think that not too many years back he had almost thrown it all away. He had never been able to figure out what had made him so stupid. He thanked God every day that Mona had been able to forgive him. He never ceased trying to make it up to her. He just didn't know how he'd live without her.

Mona was a little nervous when she went in to see Dr. Chris. Most everything was routine, but she was still a little apprehensive. She couldn't exactly define how she felt, but it was like she knew that something was not quite right. Dr. Chris did a pelvic examination, took a pap smear, and waited for her to dress to talk with her. She still had a mammogram to do, but he wanted to talk to her first. Of course, it would be a few days before the result of the pap test would come back. Dr. Chris questioned her about her eating habits, any aches and pains, but the only thing she could tell him was that she had seemed unusually depressed and felt like crying a lot of times. When he asked her if anything was bothering her, she just said nothing special. No way could she tell him about a baby who had been dead for eighteen years but wasn't dead at all. He'd think she had lost her mind, and there were times that she felt she had indeed gone crazy. To tell Dr. Chris that his head nurse and friend, Leslie, had had a baby in this very hospital and buried it nearby, but in fact the wrong baby had been buried and Leslie had an eighteen-year-old going by a different name and calling another woman Mama. Whatever would Dr. Chris say then about what was depressing her? No, she couldn't say anything. She tried to concentrate on the good things in her life, Cynthia and Patrick and Michael Jacob. They were all so important and loving to her. Why weren't they enough? Why did she have to always remember that other baby? Sometimes she felt that she was going completely out of her mind. What if she was wrong, and Angel had really died? What if it was just coincidence that Mary Ann was the spitting image of Leslie? But what about the same rare blood type—Mary Ann and Leslie? What about when she actually saw Miss Morgan move the babies' cribs? Of course, if she had had any good response from Dr. Williams all those years ago, maybe this could have been settled then, but what of the consequences? How would Steve have reacted to a child he never knew existed, and how would Mary Ann have felt about suddenly finding out her parents were not her parents, and how would the Lamberts feel, knowing the daughter they loved was not, in fact, their daughter at all? It all started with Miss Morgan, but look at the pain it would cause all the innocent people. And most important, how would it affect Leslie to have buried a child that wasn't her Angel at all? Somehow Mona realized she would have to bury the past and once and for all let Angel rest in peace.

When Mona left Dr. Chris's office and went for her mammogram, she was in better spirits. She hoped she had come to terms with her thoughts and that she could shake off some of these depressed feelings. After her mammogram, she went to meet Leslie for lunch. It would be sometime later that she'd get the results of her tests, and she was glad they were over. Dr. Chris told her he'd call her when the results were in. She breathed a sigh of relief and was feeling her old self again when she saw Leslie approaching. She marveled at how beautiful Leslie was. Her years with Steve had put a real bloom on her. Leslie loved her work and always seemed to find time for it and Steve and the children. When the four of them were together, you could readily see that Cynthia was daddy's girl and Patrick all Leslie's. She had so much to be thankful for, and seeing her Leslie cleared her mind of all the conflicting thoughts. Bob would be glad she had this doctor's visit behind her. She knew he had been concerned about her.

As soon as Leslie was seated, they ordered, and Leslie began to ask Mona about her tests. Mona assured her everything had gone well. As they ate, they made plans to get together for a family dinner real soon. Leslie would check with Jacob and find out when he and Emily could come. Mona needed to have the family around her. This would surely get rid of any depressing thoughts. She felt like she had gotten through her tests with flying colors. The results were just routine.

Chapter 40

The early morning ringing of the telephone was nothing new. Mona and Bob were both early risers, but for some reason, as Mona went to pick up the phone, she had an ominous feeling. She and Bob were just finishing their coffee, and she was a little perturbed at this insistent interruption. She loved the mornings with Bob. It was their special time together. When she said hello, she was a little surprised to hear a female voice say, "Mrs. Edwards, hold just a moment please for Dr. Chris." After Dr. Chris greeted her, he apologized for the early call, but he wanted to see her in his office this morning. It seemed there were some irregularities in her tests. No, he didn't want to discuss it on the phone. He just wanted to be sure she came in right away. Puzzled and a little nervous, she told Bob what Dr. Chris had said, which was actually nothing. Bob told her he would come with her, but she insisted that he go on to work. She'd probably have to have another test or something. It surely wasn't anything to worry about. Anyway, Leslie would be there, and she'd call him as soon as she knew anything to tell him.

Their morning had been spoiled, so Mona gathered up the dishes, put things away, and hastily cleaned up the kitchen before she went to bathe and get dressed to go back to the hospital. She felt a little out of sorts at this inconvenience. Maybe it was the nagging question of what was going on here? It couldn't be anything too serious, or Dr. Chris would have told her. She tried not to let her imagination run away with her as she chose a pair of navy slacks and a slip-over sweater to wear. These would be easy to remove if she had to undress for more tests, she thought. Maybe she'd get another chance to see Leslie for lunch. She had so enjoyed the last one. She never seemed to see enough of Leslie or Jacob. They were so busy with their own families that at times she felt like they were going farther and farther away from her. She smiled at her image in the mirror as she thought about Cynthia and Patrick and Michael Jacob. She was so lucky to have such beautiful, healthy grandchildren. She recalled when each of them was born and how precious they all were.

When Mona arrived at the hospital, one of the nurses

told her Dr. Chris was waiting to see her. Well, this was a change. She didn't have to do the waiting. When she entered Dr. Chris's office, Leslie was there, also. She smiled nervously as she greeted her and became a little more anxious to know what was going on. Dr. Chris explained that he had asked Leslie to be present, but she would leave if Mona wanted her to. Mona reached for Leslie's hand and said, "I'd like her to be here. I never really see enough of her." Dr. Chris told her he'd like to show her her mammogram, and he pointed out an oblong dark area. It looked rough, but Mona couldn't tell much about it. Dr. Chris explained that this looked like some kind of deposit, not a lump that could be felt. The right breast looked clear, but the left one had this spot. He explained that he couldn't tell exactly what it was. The only way to do that was a biopsy. It would necessitate an operation to simply remove the area for testing. He said it didn't follow the classic signs of a malignant tumor, but he felt further investigation was necessary. Mona was in shock. Breast cancer—she was sure of it. No matter what Dr. Chris said. He couldn't tell. That's why he had asked Leslie to be there. What had she ever done to deserve this? How would Bob feel if they took off her breast? She'd be a freak before she died. She struggled to hold back the tears as all these thoughts raced through her mind. Leslie was speaking softly to her, "It's okay, Mom. They simply need to pinpoint that deposit and cut it out. Then they can tell if it's malignant or not." She'd probably nothing to be alarmed about, but it had to go. She promised to be with her and said they should schedule it immediately, probably tomorrow morning. Mona couldn't believe this was happening to her. Of course, they could schedule her tomorrow, but she needed time to collect herself. How could she tell Bob and Jacob that she was probably dying of cancer? She was too young for this to happen. She would never see her grandchildren grow up, never spend the golden years with Bob. That dreaded word cancer kept ringing in her ears. She had to get control of herself. She couldn't let Leslie and Dr. Chris see her falling to pieces. She tried to put on a confident face and agreed that tomorrow would be fine for the surgery. Dr. Chris gave her instructions not to eat or drink anything after midnight and to check into the hospital at 6:30 A.M. Now she would go to the laboratory for blood tests and an EKG.

After these were finished, it would be time for lunch, and Leslie would call Jacob to join them. Everything was happening so fast. She had to get her thoughts under control. She couldn't let Leslie or Jacob see how scared she really was. There was time enough to worry if the biopsy proved to be malignant. She breathed deeply and said, "Well, let's get on with it." She asked Leslie to call her father and explain everything to him. She didn't think she could tell Bob right now and not go to pieces. By the time she got home, she could have herself under control.

Mona's lunch with Leslie and Jacob was, to say the least, subdued. Both of the children tried to make light of the problem, assuring her everything would be okay. They talked about the grandchildren, reminding her of the many cute and touching things that Cynthia, Patrick, and Michael Jacob had been involved in. They laughed a lot, but it was obvious that sometimes the laughter came close to being tears. Both Leslie and Jacob assured Mona they would be present in the morning. Leslie had already talked to Bob, so he would have time to adjust to the situation by the time Mona got home. They were all a little nervous and frightened. They hoped they could hide their fears from Mona. Leslie knew she had enough of her own.

As Mona backed out of the parking lot, she was thinking of all the family, and Angel kept looming foremost in her mind. She was the only person who knew Angel was alive, and she wouldn't even get to see her again. No one would ever know that this was Leslie's baby and her grandchild after she was dead. And with cancer, one never knew how long you might live. She wasn't really afraid of dying, but she did so want to stay with Bob a while longer, and she wanted to see the grandchildren grow up and maybe even one day have great-grandchildren. She and Bob had been through a lot in their lives. Now was just the beginning of the truly comfortable years. Somehow this didn't seem quite fair. She tried to concentrate on Dr. Chris's words when he told her he felt she'd be okay, but the surgery was the only way to be sure.

When she reached Melrose Avenue, she took a right turn. This would take her by the Warren High School, home of the Pirates. This was where Angel went to school. It was time for school to let out, and maybe Mona could get a look at her. It had been some years since she had seen her, but today she just felt like she had to. She parked near the front gate where all the children came out. The schoolyard was crowded with students, and her eyes kept darting from one to the other, looking hard so as not to miss her. The students, were yelling and waving to one another, but there was still no sign of that face that forever stayed in her mind. She was beginning to despair that she wouldn't see her when just a glimpse of that glossy hair caught her eye. Coming down the steps were these two girls, one a pretty brunette, laughing and talking with her Angel. In the years she hadn't changed at all. The same beautiful face and radiant hair and the doll-like figure. It was Leslie all over and over again. Mona slumped down in her seat and watched the girls walk by, hearing the musical sound of their laughter. She couldn't die and not tell anyone, but if she told, a lot of lives would be changed forever. She would try to put it out of her mind until the surgery was over. She vowed that then she would decide what she had to do. Now she had to get home and tell Bob that her life might nearly be over. One never knew what one day could bring. This morning she had been so happy and content, and now she was facing another crisis in her life, one that might kill her.

Chapter 41

The day had been long and very disturbing to Leslie. She tried to reassure herself as she had Mona, that this was just a biopsy to rule out any possibility of a malignancy. It was the prudent thing to do. Dr. Chris was hopeful, and she knew he was right, but she couldn't put away that nagging fear that her mother could have cancer. Cancer wasn't really the end of the world, but Leslie had seen too many patients die with some form of cancer and not any of them pretty. She would be glad to get home and talk to Steve. He was always so level-headed, and she needed his reassurance. She couldn't imagine what she would do if something happened to Mona. They had been through so much together, and Mona had always been there for her, never judging her, nor blaming her, just there to help her. Sometimes she forgot what a really good person her mother was, but the slightest indication that she might lose her was totally devastating. In fact, it just couldn't happen.

By the time Steve arrived home, Leslie had worked herself into quite a stew. Cynthia and Patrick were playing with the neighbors' children, and she was trying to think about dinner. She had made the salad, and the chicken had cooked all day in the crock pot. She only needed to put the scalloped potatoes in the microwave, and she would be all set for dinner when Steve arrived. Leslie had learned a long time ago how to utilize her crock pot and her microwave. They both saved her a lot of time and work.

She heard Steve drive up and then the happy voices as Cynthia and Patrick greeted their father. Both were talking at once trying to tell Steve of the day's events. She could hardly wait herself to talk to him alone about her mom. That would have to be after dinner and after the children had gone to their rooms. No use upsetting them. Time enough for that if their worst fears were justified.

Smiling as he entered the house, both kids clinging to his arms, he came over to give Leslie a hug. He was happy to be greeted by the kids. He loved them so, and as he looked at Leslie, he thought, "What a lucky man I am!" He and Jacob had really done well in the business, and he just couldn't see any dark cloud anywhere. Everything was so perfect, it was almost scary. Leslie smiled at him, but Steve caught a fleeting glimpse of something not quite right. Well, he'd be patient. If anything was wrong, Leslie would tell him. Even the little things at work that she felt were her fault, she told him. Together they could solve any problem, and if one of them was distressed, the other one could reason away their fears. Yes, he was the luckiest man in the world to have Leslie and the children.

As soon as the kids had gone to their rooms and the kitchen was cleaned up, Leslie and Steve took their favorite chairs in the living room. Steve waited patiently. He knew Leslie had something serious on her mind—at least, serious to her. Sometimes things Leslie took for serious turned out to be nothing at all in the clear light of thinking. Finally Leslie broke the silence and said, "Steve, my mother may have cancer." Steve straightened up in his chair and waited for her to continue. "Her mammogram showed a large deposit in her left breast. Of course, there's no way of knowing for sure what it is until it's removed. Mom is going into surgery first thing in the morning." Steve was stunned! He went over to take Leslie in his arms, and she cried softly against his shoulder. He tried to reassure her, but he felt a little helpless. This was Leslie's field, not his, and she certainly knew more of the implications than he did. She went on to say that Dr. Chris was especially hopeful. He really didn't think it was malignant. It wasn't the classic tumor characteristically, but of course he couldn't be sure.

Steve said, "Leslie, I'll be there with you tomorrow, and we'll look only for the best. No use borrowing trouble. You trust Dr. Chris's opinion, and he's probably right. Just look on the bright side. We all love Mona, and you know the whole family will be there praying for her. She needs our support because it must also be very scary for her." With that, Steve picked up the phone to call Mona. When she answered the phone, Steve said, "Leslie has told me the problem. Don't worry. We will all be there for you tomorrow. We love you, Mona, and we're not going to let anything bad happen to you."

Tears rushed to Mona's eyes, but she was able to keep her voice light as she talked to Steve. "Yes," she said, "I am a little worried, but I have every reason to believe everything will be okay. No one in my family has ever had cancer, and Dr. Chris is hopeful."

What Steve didn't know was that Bob had been late at the office and had just arrived home. Mona was on the verge of talking to him when the phone rang. As Mona hung up the phone, she turned to Bob and said, "That was Steve offering his good wishes for tomorrow. I'm going into surgery at 6:30 in the morning to have a spot removed from my breast." With that she broke down and cried deep sobs which racked her body. Bob was in shock and held her in his arms until finally she lay quietly.

"Now tell me all about it," he said. She had finally let loose the torrent of tears she had held back, so she was not able to relay to Bob very well all that had transpired that day. She kept wondering out loud what it would be like if she had to have her breast removed, or even both, if it had spread. Bob was grim as he tried to take in all that Mona told him. He had left home this morning on top of the world, and this evening of the same day found him trying to find some way to comfort Mona. "Don't you know I love you with or without your breasts? From what you've told me, I have to believe everything is going to be all right. We will all be there for you tomorrow, and then we'll know the next step—if there is a next step. I wish you had called me so I could have been with you sooner. There's nothing quite like being alone and letting your imagination run away with you. I'm sure Dr. Winslow will do the surgery, but you know Dr. Chris will be right there. We'll have to leave early to be at the hospital by 6:30. I'm sure this is so they will have time to prepare you for surgery. Let's go to bed now. You'll need your rest. Try not to worry, darling, we'll all be with you."

Chapter 42

Among the last students to leave the high school building were Tonya and Mary Ann. They had stayed late to finish some work on the school paper. It seemed there was never enough time to catch up on everything. Being seniors kept them busy. Tonya always told Mary Ann that she had to study harder just to keep up with her, and in a way, it was true. It seemed to Tonya that Mary Ann knew all the answers without even opening a book, but she really didn't have to study much. Most things were easy for her to remember. Today, however, Tonya had stayed to help Mary Ann on the school paper because she wanted to talk to her about their dates for the upcoming prom and what they would wear.

As they came down the steps, they noticed a strange car parked in front. Strange because most of the students were gone already, and it was usually the same cars every day that came to pick up students. Mary Ann glanced sideways and saw this lady sort of slumped down in her seat. She didn't recognize her as someone she knew, but she looked vaguely familiar, as if she had seen her somewhere before. She said to Tonya, "I've seen that lady somewhere before, but I can't remember where. Do you know who she is?" Tonya took another look and said, "No, I've never seen her before. She obviously isn't going to pick up anyone because she's now driving away." They both looked again at the car and driver as she passed them walking down the street. It bugged Mary Ann that she couldn't remember when or where she had seen her before. It must have been a long time ago, but it kept gnawing in the back of her mind.

Both Tonya and Mary Ann were thinking about new dresses for the prom and their current boyfriends. Neither of the girls dated too much. In fact, they had lots of friends, but they were too involved in thinking of college and future plans to want a steady boyfriend. This certainly pleased both sets of parents, who had reminded them that the right person would come along at the right time. Mary Ann had accepted a date with a young man, Andrew Hawkins, captain of the basketball team. His parents were friends of her parents. She and Andrew had always gotten along really well, and he wasn't interested at present in a steady girlfriend. She enjoyed Andrew's company and knew they would have fun. Tonya was going with a jock, Mason Montgomery. Mary Ann secretly thought he was a jerk. However, she didn't tell this to Tonya. He was okay, she guessed, but his know-it-all attitude didn't match up very well with Tonya. But Mary Ann remembered how excited Tonya was when he asked her to the prom. Tonya had changed a lot since the old days with Ralph, but there were still times and situations that made her unsure of herself. Peter had given so much to Tonya. He had built up her self-esteem and had helped her to become a very self-sufficient young lady. Tonya was delighted when Mason invited her to the prom. She knew she was the envy of a number of other girls. She also knew Mary Ann wasn't too impressed with Mason. She hadn't said anything, but Tonya could tell. She would have felt better if Mary Ann had liked Mason because they would be spending a lot of time together, but in any case, they both expected to have a super evening.

Right now the idea of new prom dresses was uppermost in their minds. Joan and Hannah were going shopping with them on Saturday, but the girls were already fixing in their minds what kind of dresses they wanted. Tonya was thinking of red to set off her olive skin and brown hair. Mary Ann was thinking of a blue to match her eyes. Both girls preferred the short length because it made for easier dancing. Papa wasn't too keen about the real short length, but he usually allowed Joan and Mary Ann to decide where to draw the line. He didn't want to sound like an old fuddy duddy, but seeing the college girls every day in skirts too short to sit down in had prejudiced him in favor of a longer length. He often wanted to warn Mary Ann against such wearing apparel, but so far he hadn't needed to say anything. He and Joan had agreed years ago to give Mary Ann certain freedoms. They would teach her their values and allow her to find her own. So far, she had not disappointed them. Mary Ann often asked his advice, and he had not faltered in advising her, but so far he had not found it necessary to force his viewpoint on her.

Every day Paul thanked God, who in His infinite wisdom, had given Mary Ann to them to raise at a time when they had almost given up hope. He had always been a Christian and believed in God's goodness, but never more so than when Joan gave birth to their darling Mary Ann. Paul would never forget that marvelous feeling of a miracle when the doctor had finally pronounced Mary Ann out of danger. Never would he forget the hours he stood outside the nursery and prayed for that tiny being trying so hard to live. He would never forget that little baby face. Oh, she'd grown up to be a remarkably pretty young woman, but he would always see her lying in that baby crib just waiting to go home with him and Joan. He could hardly believe that time had passed so quickly. It seemed only yesterday that he had watched Mary Ann go to school for the very first time. Now in a short while she would be graduating from high school and then going off to college. He tried not to think of the empty house, no one to come rushing to meet him, throwing her arms around him, and calling him Papa. When she had first called him Papa, he had thought it would pass and she'd call him Daddy or Dad, but she had stayed with Papa and the way she said it always made him feel special. That term wasn't often used anymore, and at first Joan had teased him, saying it made him sound old, but later they both cherished the term, knowing it belonged only to him. What incredible joy Mary Ann had brought to their lives. He saw students every day, all kinds, and it made him even more aware of how special Mary Ann really was—her sensitivity, her concern for others, her optimism, always looking for the best, and her never-failing loyalty. These were just a few of the things he saw in her. She didn't realize what a truly beautiful young woman she had become. When he watched her helping Joan around the house, he had to swallow hard to keep down the lump that kept forming and to fight back the tears—tears of gratitude and joy for this young woman who was his child, his own flesh and blood. In Mary Ann he saw more clearly what this world is truly all about.

Chapter 43

The ringing of the alarm clock startled Mona. It really didn't wake her because she had been lying there awake. It seemed she barely dozed all night. So many thoughts kept going through her mind, and no amount of rationalizing could erase that dreaded fear that she had cancer. She kept thinking of the financial drain at a time when they were feeling comfortable about Bob being able to cut back on his work. The emotional strain of taking care of someone with cancer, knowing that sooner or later it would kill the one you loved, and the quiet anguish of looking at your family, knowing you would be leaving them far too soon. Her body felt bone weary from turning and tossing, but it was her mind that was in torment. She slowly sat up on the side of the bed, knowing she had allowed herself just enough time to get to the hospital by 6:30. Bob was already in the shower. She wished for a cup of coffee, but she could only rinse her mouth with water. Nothing to eat or drink this morning.

Mona had packed a small bag with a couple of nightgowns and toiletries just in case she needed them. When she worked at the hospital, she had noticed a lot of patients wearing hospital gowns. In any case, she was prepared. She hurriedly dressed and took a last look around as Bob carried her bag to the car. After today, her life might be changed forever, and she wanted to firmly engrave in her mind the way things were before. It was like walking into the unknown, not wanting to go for fear of what lay ahead, but also knowing you had no choice but to make the best of whatever you found waiting for you. She said a prayer, "God, please take care of me," as she closed the door behind her.

There was already a hustle-bustle atmosphere around the hospital when she arrived. She saw breakfast carts, cleaning people, and of course the nurses scurrying about. As soon as she checked in she was taken to a room so she could start being prepared. She got the usual enema, and an IV was put in her arm. When she was situated in bed, in a hospital gown, the family was able to see her. Leslie and Steve and Jacob and Emily were all there as she knew they would be, and she felt a little guilty at having totally disrupted their day. Leslie's duty

179

didn't begin until 7:30, but she had wanted to see Mona before she began her day. Of course, she would be with her in the recovery room as soon as the surgery ended, but Dr. Chris had told her he preferred her not to be in surgery. She had wanted to be with her mother all the way, but she knew Dr. Chris was right. She could stay with her, however, in recovery.

They all tried to smile and put on good faces and kept reassuring Mona that everything would be fine. Bob gave her a kiss as the nurse came to take her down to the mammogram room. The pathologist, Dr. Allen, had to pinpoint the spot in her breast and would run a wire down to its center. The nurse wheeled her first to see a video of exactly what Dr. Allen would be doing. Mona tried to watch, but she suddenly felt dizzy as if she were going to faint. She tried to speak to the nurse, but it was as if she were a long way off. The nurse saw her turn pale and quickly took her back to her room and helped her onto the bed. Mona's blood pressure had shot up, and she felt sick. After a short time lying down, she began to feel okay again, and the nurse told her, "We'll try it again, but this time we'll go straight to Dr. Allen."

As Mona sat on the high stool that placed her breast even with the machine, she had all sorts of misgivings. This wasn't part of the surgery, this was just getting her ready. It felt like her breast was being pulled out of its socket as it was clamped down for the mammogram. It wasn't really painful, but most certainly uncomfortable. After her breast was released, Dr. Allen took a needle and ran it from the top of the breast to the lower part, trying to pinpoint the center of the deposit. Then another picture was taken to see if it was right. This went on for what seemed like two hours. It was actually only forty-five minutes. It took three tries before the needle was in the right place. Then he inserted a wire and dye into the spot so it was marked for the surgeon. By this time, Mona felt again like she might faint. Sweat poured off her face, and she felt clammy all over. When the gurney finally arrived so she could lie down, she welcomed it. She much preferred surgery to what she had just been through. As she was wheeled into the operating room, she kept her eyes closed and again wondered if this was the beginning of the end!

Grim faced, Bob, Steve, Emily, and Jacob all sat in the

waiting room not saying much, each with their own thoughts, waiting for Leslie to bring them any news of Mona. They didn't know she had been forty-five minutes in the lab before going to surgery. Leslie had gone with Mona to the operating room door. There she had kissed her mother and assured her she would be waiting in recovery. Leslie had still wanted to be in surgery, but Dr. Chris had refused her request. She often helped in surgery, and Dr. Chris liked working with her, but he had told Leslie, "Not this time—not when it's your mom. I know you are a professional, Leslie, but no one needs to work on their own family." Leslie knew he was right, but it didn't make it any easier to be outside waiting. She said a prayer for Mona and went back to the waiting room to report to the family what was going on, then she went to the recovery room to see that everything was ready when Mona came in. Waiting was the hardest part.

As Mona looked at the bright light above the operating table, heard the nurses and doctors talking, and watched their ghost-like figures moving around, she felt like she was in another world. She was groggy and everything was a little foggy. She knew she hadn't been given the anesthesia yet, but already she had the sense of being far away in space and everything was dreamlike. Dr. Winslow spoke to her, telling her they were about ready to start. Then he told her, "Mona, we are going to put you to sleep now." And she had a sudden taste of garlic in her mouth just before nothing . . .

She heard noises and she wanted to open her eyes, but the lids were too heavy. She thought she heard Leslie's voice speaking to her, and she wanted to answer, but the words wouldn't come. She tried to take a deep breath, but as she did she felt a stabbing pain in her breast. She knew she had had surgery, but she couldn't quite figure out where she was now. A little later she clearly heard Leslie's voice saying, "Mom, can you hear me?" She wanted to nod her head, but she couldn't move. She did finally move her lips. She wasn't sure if there was any sound. Apparently Leslie had understood because she began to talk to her telling where the family was waiting for her. Sometime last night Mona had come to a decision. Regardless of the outcome of her surgery, she was going to tell Leslie about Angel. Someone other than herself had to know the truth. Even as she lay in recovery, this again crossed her mind, and she was even more certain that she could not go to her grave burying this secret with her. Someone else had to know that Angel lived.

Slowly, she was able to open her eyes, and the room and Leslie came into focus. Leslie held her hand and said, "We're going to take you to your room now." Mona coughed, and again there was a sharp pain in her breast. She tried to put her hand on the spot, but she felt something. Leslie explained that there was a tube in the incision for drainage. That was where it hurt if she so much as breathed deeply. She didn't ask Leslie about the outcome of the surgery. Dr. Chris had promised her he would tell her first the results of the surgery, good or bad. If it was malignant, she wanted to be the one to tell the family and prepare herself.

As soon as she had been put in her room and straightened in her bed, Bob came in, along with Steve, Jacob, and Emily. Mona tried to smile and assure them she was okay. The surgery had gone fine, she knew that, but waiting for the results from the deposit taken out was the trying time. She thought she heard Dr. Chris's voice down the hall, and she tried to say a little prayer as she waited for him to give her the good or bad news. The very thought of cancer struck a note of terror in her heart, and as the door swung open, she knew the next few minutes would seal her fate.

Chapter 44

All eyes were on Dr. Chris as he came into the room and walked over to Mona's bed. He took her hand and said, "Mona, it's okay. The biopsy was negative. There is no malignancy. You were lucky we found it, however; that deposit was a perfect breeding ground for cancer." Everyone was smiling, but the tears she had held back came gushing down Mona's face. She had been so afraid, but now, thank God, she could just concentrate on getting over the surgery, and she'd be her old self again. Dr. Chris went on explaining to her that the tube would come out the next day, and in a couple of days she could go home.

Mona had such a feeling of relief, and she suddenly felt so sleepy, as if she could sleep for a week. She had been a bundle of nerves and hadn't really rested at all before coming to the hospital. Leslie could see how Mona felt, and she suggested to Jacob, Emily, Steve, and Bob that they might want to go out for lunch and give Mona a chance to rest. They readily agreed. They were so relieved; it was like a heavy weight had been lifted off their shoulders. They all said goodbye to Mona, and Bob assured her he would be back soon.

As soon as the others left, Leslie straightened Mona's pillows and told her she should sleep now. She would be close by if she should need anything. She kissed her mother on the cheek and squeezed her hand as they gazed into each other's eyes. Mona said, "Leslie, we can thank God today. He has given me a new lease on life. I hope I can be worthy and can be a better person. Surely God has a purpose for sparing me and allowing me to continue to watch my grandchildren grow and to spend more of my years with your father. I'm so very lucky to have all of you." And with a smile on her face, Mona drifted off into a peaceful sleep as Leslie watched and then quietly left the room.

Mona woke startled as another sharp pain shot through her breast. Obviously she had moved in her sleep. For the first time since returning to her room, she felt awake enough to look around. This was a private room with windows along one side allowing sunlight to illuminate the room. Everything was painted an off-white with mint-green drapes. A bedside table held kleenex, a small book, and a bottle of body lotion. An IV stand stood at the head of the bed, and Mona could see the slow drip from the bag as it went into her arm. It didn't really hurt, but sometimes her arm became stiff because she couldn't move it too much. A television was on a hanging rack in line with her bed. On a bedrail that pulled up on the side was a telephone. This was the first time in years Mona had been in the hospital except to visit, and although she had done a lot of volunteer work here, she had never really scrutinized the room as she did now. Well, if you must be sick, this was a nice place. She noticed one door that must be the closet. The one left ajar was the bathroom.

She rang for the nurse. She needed to go to the bathroom and didn't think she could make it by herself with the IV bottle. The nurse helped her to sit up, but Mona had to place one hand under her breast to stop the pain. She wasn't particularly large busted, but the slightest sag caused pains to shoot through her. Holding her breast up, and with the nurse holding the IV bottle, Mona managed to hobble to the bathroom. It must have been a funny sight, but Mona was afraid to laugh; the slightest jar brought on the pain. She thought it would help if she could put on her bra to support her breast, but until the tube came out, this wasn't possible. Knowing she didn't have cancer, Mona's sense of humor returned, and she tried to see herself in a comic situation. It took all her strength just to walk the short distance to the bathroom, and she was totally exhausted when she finally got straightened out in her bed.

She noticed a lovely bouquet of red roses, obviously they had been delivered while she was sleeping. She suspected they were from Bob, although she couldn't see the card. Most of her friends didn't know she was in the hospital. It had all happened so fast, and it had been too scary to even talk about. She had meant to call her minister, but she had really only wanted her family around her. Lying there, knowing she was going to be okay, allowed her the luxury of planning for the future. There were the things she and Bob had wanted to do as he shortened his workload, and there were the things they wanted to do next summer with the grandchildren. Thinking of grandchildren brought back Angel to mind and her firm resolve to tell Leslie the truth. What if she had had cancer and died? Then no one would have known of Angel's existence. What if she were in an accident and had no time left to tell Leslie? She simply had to tell her. She should have done it from the beginning. Leslie would have to decide how she would handle it. Mona realized only too well that the innocent often suffer the pain, and certainly Angel was innocent, as were the Lamberts, who believed Angel was their child, and Leslie, who believed her child was dead, and Steve the father, who didn't even know he was the father. All would suffer the pain of the innocent if the truth were known to all parties. In spite of everything and the far-reaching effects on Leslie and Steve and on Cynthia and Patrick, and also Angel, she could no longer carry the burden alone. It was indeed a Pandora's box, and she would have to face the responsibility of raising its lid. She'd tell Leslie when she was out of the hospital and well again.

Mona dozed intermittently and tried not to make any sudden moves. She wondered why they didn't invent a sling for the breast as they had for a broken arm. The incision was at the top of her breast, and from this a coil of tube protruded. Any slight movement of the tube brought on sharp pains. It was an awkward position to be in, as well as painful. It was extremely difficult to change her position, and sometimes she felt that she just had to move a little. Bob came back to sit with her. He had insisted that Jacob and Steve go back to work, and Emily had gone to check on the children. Mona was glad they were alone for a few minutes. Time to count their blessings. She couldn't begin to tell Bob how scared she had been, and he admitted to being petrified at the thought of her having cancer. That was over now, and in a couple of weeks, she'd be good as new.

Leslie went past her mother's room and smiled to herself as she saw her father sitting by the bed, holding her mother's hand. They were such a good-looking couple and still so devoted to each other after all these years. She hoped it would always be like this for her and Steve. She couldn't even imagine life without him. With Steve, Cynthia, and Patrick, life couldn't be more wonderful. In spite of the trials of the past, all that was way behind her; she couldn't even ask for a better life. In fact, it was perfect—not a cloud on the horizon. Now that her mom was going to be okay, she really felt good. She was going in to visit her mom soon, but now she just wanted her dad to have a chance to be alone with her for a while.

As night drew near, Mona insisted that Bob go home. He needed to rest, and she would probably get to go home tomorrow afternoon. The tube was supposed to come out in the morning. Bob reluctantly agreed. He did feel beat, so he kissed her good night and headed for home. This had been a long day for all of them.

Leslie was accustomed to being tired by the end of the day, and this was no exception. She was bone tired, but with a happy feeling. It had really been a scare about her mother, but now that she knew it was not malignant she felt a feeling of relief. She didn't like to think how scared she had really been. She knew they had come a long way in breast cancer treatment. It could buy some time, but it seemed to her that, in the end, cancer always won out. Dr. Chris had assured her that Mona did well in surgery and would probably go home tomorrow afternoon. With all these positive thoughts, Leslie went in to say good night to her mother. It was time for Leslie to go home, and she was anxious to reassure Cynthia and Patrick that their grandmother was doing just fine. All they knew was that Mona was going to be in the hospital for a couple of days. As Leslie said goodbye, she assured Mona she would see her first thing in the morning. She still had the IV in her arm, and a nurse came in with a pill for her. She hoped it would help her sleep through the night. This day had been a traumatic one, but thanks to God, it had a good ending. All she wanted to do now was sleep. She'd worry about other things later.

As planned, Mona went home the very next day from the hospital, and as her spirits soared, so did her physical being start to return to normal. Bob insisted she really take it easy and she did, but nothing could slow down the elated feeling she had, just knowing that she was okay, and the dreaded word cancer had not applied to her. She had felt so sure that this was her fate and so grateful to God for sparing her. It revived her and filled her with such a feeling of joy and well-being, one she couldn't begin to explain. Perhaps this had been a warning to get her house in order, to do the things she knew she must, and finally set free the secret that only she knew. More and more, Mona realized that it was absolutely imperative that she talk to Leslie. Somehow, she had to make Leslie understand why she had been silent so long. She had to trust God to show her the way and

186

give her the strength to finally admit the truth. Leslie might even hate her for hiding Angel from her for eighteen years. She might never speak to her again. In acknowledging a grandchild, she might lose her own daughter, and in turn Cynthia and Patrick. Even Bob, who had always supported her, might not understand. She went over and over all these things in her mind, but in the end, she knew there was no other way. Whatever the outcome, she had to tell Leslie the truth.

Chapter 45

The night of the prom finally arrived, and Mary Ann was thrilled and excited as Joan helped her to get dressed. Sure enough, Mary Ann had found the perfect dress, blue of course, to match her eyes, spaghetti straps with a fitted bodice and full skirt. Not too short, but knee length. She knew Papa's feelings about too short and tight. And although he hadn't said any-thing, she wanted him to be proud of her. Joan had brushed her shoulder-length hair until it glowed and crackled, and then fas-tened her own pearls around Mary Ann's neck. As she looked at her daughter, so beautiful, Joan's eyes filled with tears. Not tears of sadness, but of joy and pride and love that only a mother can feel for her child. They quietly hugged and then went to find Papa so he could see how she looked before Andrew came to pick her up.

Andrew had agreed to pick her up a little early along with Mason, and together they would pick up Tonya. Mason hadn't seemed too happy to go along with Andrew and Mary Ann, but they had managed to convince him that Mary Ann and Tonya wanted to be together and that the four of them would have a really good time.

Mary Ann knew how beautiful Tonya would look. Her dress was red and accented her olive skin, dark hair, and eyes. Like Mary Ann, Tonya loved to dance, and she was a good dancer. Hannah helped Tonya get dressed, and both she and Peter smiled happily as they admired Tonya's appearance and the excitement that glowed in her eyes. They were both delight-ed that she and Mason were double dating with Mary Ann and Andrew. They didn't know Mason all that well, just that he was a handsome athlete and that Tonya was delighted he had asked her to the prom.

So many things had been happening lately—the final weeks of school, the waiting to see who the valedictorian would be (there were several students very close to the top), getting ready for the graduation ceremonies, and tonight the prom for which they had waited so long.

When Mary Ann, Andrew, and Mason arrived to pick up Tonya, they all came in so they could admire one another and greet Hannah and Peter before they left. They were all quite handsome, and Tonya and Mary Ann hugged as they admired each other. They were going to dinner before they went to the prom, but Tonya was sure she wouldn't be able to eat a bite. This was all such fun. They said goodbye to Hannah and Peter and happily drove away with Andrew at the wheel.

Tonya had dated some before, but tonight was different, and Hannah couldn't help but have a little anxious feeling. Peter tried to reassure her, teasing her a little about not wanting her baby to grow up. Hannah knew Peter was right, but couldn't quite shake an uneasy feeling. She did have to admit no one could have looked more beautiful than Tonya nor more hand-some than Mason. They were certainly a striking couple, and this was the night long awaited.

It was hard for Mary Ann to even imagine that they were actually seniors and getting ready for college. She had expected and even looked forward to this day, but now that the time was here, she felt a little sad. Looking back through the years, the closeness to Tonya had been wonderful. Even when she ripped her arm, and later the surgery that had removed the scar, wasn't all that bad. Tonight she felt like the fairy princess, and the years before simply led up to this happy occasion. After the prom was graduation. And she was finally all grown up. She wondered if Tonya was feeling as she did—all happy and excited and a little sad, too. Things were already beginning to change. She and Tonya would be going to different colleges, and there would be new friends. Tonight was not really the time to think of all these things. Tonight was the time for enjoying the fun, the dancing, and being with Andrew, Tonya, and Mason.

Chapter 46

As the days crept slowly by, Mona became more and more convinced she had to have a talk with Leslie. Physically, she had healed, but mentally she was in a terrible turmoil. No turning back now, she simply had to tell Leslie the truth. But what was the truth? Could she be mistaken? No, there was no mistake. Every time she closed her eyes she saw Angel. It wasn't Mary Ann Lambert. It was Leslie's Angel. No question in her mind about that. Leslie might never speak to her again for not telling her years ago, but no matter the consequences, Leslie had to finally know the truth.

Mona dialed the hospital, and when Leslie was on the phone, she told her she needed to talk to her privately. No Bob and no Steve. And they decided to meet at a small restaurant for dinner. Leslie was a bit puzzled, but she could afford to humor her mom. After all they had been through, Mona was entitled to be a bit mysterious. She called Steve and explained she was meeting her mom after work. She asked him to look after Patrick and Cynthia and said she'd be home as early as she could. She explained that Mona was a bit mysterious, but sometimes postoperative patients became a little depressed and needed cheering up. She'd tell him all about it when she came home. Steve would wait up for her.

Mona had called Bob to explain she was going out with Leslie, and with a determined sigh, she hurriedly took a shower and dressed. She was still torn somewhat over what she was planning to do, so she tried not to think, but simply went through the motions of getting ready to go. She was apprehensive and nervous as she drove to Warren and wondered if it had been a good idea to meet Leslie at the restaurant. She expected to take a back booth, away from the main room and the noise. As she pulled into the parking lot, she spied Leslie's car. Well, it was certainly no time to get cold feet. She had made up her mind, and she wouldn't bail out now.

Leslie was waiting in a small back booth and stood to give her a hug. Leslie looked so pretty and happy, Mona thought, and she was about to be responsible for taking that smile off her face. The waitress brought them both iced tea, and Leslie said, "Mom, I've already ordered for both of us. I still

191

remember what you always like best here." After the waitress left, Leslie said, "Mom, what do you want to talk about, or do you want to wait until after we eat? I'll admit you sounded a bit mysterious, and I'm curious." Mona took a deep breath and said, "Leslie, I don't really know where or how to begin, but please hear me out before you say anything. What I'm going to tell you will sound preposterous and impossible, but I assure you that I'm convinced of its truth. If you remember on the day Angel was born, there was another child born premature who was in the same room with her. As I looked through the glass, I saw Miss Morgan take off the wristbands and change places with the beds. I thought nothing of it at the time, and then we were told Angel died. Our grief and devastation at burying our Angel erased that scene from my mind. Six years later, you remember you gave blood for a little girl who slashed her arm on a slide at school. She had the same rare blood type as you. That child was Mary Ann Lambert, the baby born the same day as Angel. I was reading to the children at the hospital that day and happened to go into her room. What I saw made me suddenly ill, and I had to go to the washroom to compose myself. That child sitting in the bed was you, Leslie, from the blue eyes, the golden hair, the smile, and the same tilt of your head. When I returned to her room, she had gone, but for days it haunted me. The picture of Miss Morgan moving the babies kept coming back to my mind, so I finally went to see Dr. Williams. He, of course, praised Miss Morgan and said it was unthinkable that she would have changed places with the babies. At that time, I was convinced that the dead baby had not been our Angel, but Mary Ann Lambert. I kept wanting to put it out of my mind, but one day I saw in the paper that Mary Ann would be in a gymnastics contest here in Warren, and I went by. By this time, she was twelve years old. Believe me when I say this time, I was even more convinced. Leslie, every step she took, every toss of her head, was you at that age. Again, I tried to put it out of my mind. I told no one. I'm sure your dad would think I'm crazy. Recently, I drove by her school, and there she was. I might never have told you or anyone except when I was in the hospital, I realized that I was the only person alive who knew this, and if I died, you would never know that I believe Mary Ann Lambert is our own Angel. She will be graduating right away from high school, and we have missed eighteen years of her life. I know all the complications, but this time the decision of what to do has to be yours. I also know I risk your anger and maybe even hate that I haven't told you before. I hope you can forgive me for that."

Stunned by what Mona had told her, Leslie could only sit in silence trying to absorb all she had heard. Of course, Mona had to be wrong. Miss Morgan was a good nurse, and nothing like that could happen here at this hospital. So maybe she looked a little like me, but what Mona was saying just couldn't be true. She had held Angel and wept over her and laid her to rest. The past eighteen years she had held that memory. She could still see that precious face. What Mona was saying could not be true. Yes, she gave blood for this child, Mary Ann, but it must have been coincidence that they had the same rare blood type. Yet, Mom was so sure.

Leslie finally said to Mona, "I have to see Mary Ann." It could easily be proved whose child she really was. Then how could she ever tell Steve that he had an eighteen-year-old daughter that he never knew about? What about the girl herself, who thought she was Mary Ann Lambert, in fact had never been anyone else? Oh God, this was too much of a Pandora's box.

Mona slowly took from her purse a newspaper clipping showing the picture of a young girl who had been named vale-dictorian of her class and handed it across the table to Leslie. One look and Leslie felt like she was going to faint. It could have been herself. No denying the tilt of her head, the slant of her nose, and the eyes. Suddenly, she knew her mom was not wrong. This was her Angel. She had not died, but was living here in Warren. She had to see her, and hold her, and weep for the lost years. This was her own flesh and blood. The tiny form buried so long ago had belonged to someone else. Leslie's first impulse was to go immediately to the Lamberts' house and claim her child. She had missed so much, but of course she couldn't do that. First of all, she had to tell Steve, and together they would claim their child.

Neither Mona nor Leslie had eaten much of their dinner, but Leslie was eager to get home to tell Steve the wonderful news that Angel was actually alive. She hugged Mona, and as they said goodbye in the parking lot, she assured her that she had done the right thing and that everything would be okay. With a sigh of relief, Mona got in her car to go home as Leslie sped out the drive in a rush to tell Steve everything.

Chapter 47

Leslie jumped out of her car and almost ran to the house. Steve was waiting up for her and seemed surprised she was back so early. "My, you and Mona had a short dinner," he commented as he gave her a kiss, "but I'm glad you're home. It's always lonely without you, Leslie."

Leslie looked around for the children and said, "Steve, there's something I must tell you. It's totally incredible, and I hope you will be as excited as I am. It's very complicated and has a lot of far-reaching consequences, but in the end, I'm sure everything will be wonderful." They walked arm in arm to their bedroom and closed the door so Leslie could begin her tale.

"Steve, do you remember our very first date and what happened? I'm not bringing this up to hurt you, only so you will understand. It was the consequence of that date that I became pregnant. I wasn't aware I was pregnant until some seven months later. I gave birth to a tiny baby girl. She was so tiny, and the next day I was told she died. Mom and Dad and I had a funeral in the chapel and buried this tiny being in the nearby cemetery. We named her Angel. Only the hospital people and the three of us knew of her existence. She was beautiful. Now it seems our Angel didn't die, but another baby did. Mom believes our baby was deliberately switched for the dead baby by one of the nurses, Miss Morgan. Mom saw Miss Morgan change the beds, but at the time, she didn't know why. She believes that the baby raised as Mary Ann Lambert is really our baby, Angel. You know I have a rare blood type, and a few years ago, I gave blood for a little girl who turned out to be Mary Ann. Of course, I didn't see her, but Mom did. She began to suspect then that she was Angel, but it was only recently that she was convinced. I saw a newspaper picture of Mary Ann, and I, too, believe she has to be Angel. We need to figure out how we can claim our own daughter. We have lost so many years."

Steve listened in awe. He couldn't believe what he was hearing. Here his wife, the love of his life, was telling him that he had fathered a child some eighteen years ago, and she hadn't even bothered to tell him. He thought he knew Leslie well, but now he didn't know if he knew her at all. One of the things he loved so in Leslie was her openness and her honesty. How could she have hidden the knowledge of this baby all these years? Yes, he had made a big mistake. He had forced himself on Leslie, and he had suffered for his behavior, but why didn't she tell him? Suddenly, he had to get out. He couldn't comprehend all he had heard, and this woman telling him these things was like a stranger to him. He couldn't discuss the situation. What was there to discuss? He was supposed to be overjoyed at the news that he had been a father eighteen years ago, and no one bothered to tell him. He was supposed to run out and inform a young woman that he was really her father, although he had been in the dark as much as she had! Steve simply knew he had to leave the house. He hastily gathered a few clothes and sadly took a last look around. This room had meant so much to him and Leslie. It was more than a bedroom. It was a place for special talks and confidences, a place to bare your soul to the one you loved most in all the world. Steve felt along with his anger and disbelief, a surge of sadness overtake him as he quietly closed the door, possibly forever.

Leslie sat stricken as Steve packed his bag and left. She was devastated and fell on the bed, sobs racking her body. Never did it occur to her that Steve would be so angry. She expected surprise and even a little hurt, but not this. Had her finding Angel caused her to lose the love of her life? Was she just supposed to forget Angel, her own flesh and blood? What if she lost Cynthia or Patrick? It was the same thing. Through no fault of her own, she had lost Angel, and now she had found her. Of course, she had to claim her no matter. If Steve couldn't understand, she was sorry. In fact, she felt as if her whole world had suddenly turned upside down. What could she tell Cynthia and Patrick? That their father had left because she lied to him, not lied exactly, but had withheld the truth from him?

She knew she had to compose herself, and although she didn't expect to sleep at all, she knew she had to try. Perhaps in the morning light, things would be clearer, and she could better decide what course of action to take. She had counted so on Steve's support. He always put things in their proper perspective for her, and she couldn't bear the thought of him not being there beside her. The pain was too horrible to bear. At least until morning, she wouldn't have to explain Steve's absence to the children. Maybe by morning she could think more clearly.

As Steve drove away from his home, tears ran down his face, and he felt that he had just had a death in the family. He still couldn't believe all the things Leslie had told him. Yes, he was guilty. He had forced Leslie, and it was this act of his that had brought on all of these problems. But she could have told him. He could have accepted his responsibility, but she didn't give him a chance. Yes, that night in the car when she had said "no," he hadn't given her much of a chance, either. In all their years of marriage, that night had been put behind them. She said she forgave him, but he hadn't known just how much she had to forgive him for. Bob and Mona had been so kind to him, never letting on that he had caused such havoc in their lives.

He checked into a hotel and tried to sleep. Thoughts kept pounding his head, and he knew sleep was out of the question. He had walked out on Leslie tonight. He wasn't there for her when she needed him. Maybe it was his own guilt that had made him blame her so strongly for keeping the secret of Angel. When Angel was born, he was still an irresponsible student. What would he have done if she had told him? Perhaps the upsetting of his perfect family and his perfect life was the main problem. He was so happy and content with his life just the way it was. Now everything was changed. He also realized that he was no longer an irresponsible boy, but a grown man who had to face up to his own responsibilities, not run away from them. He couldn't imagine what Leslie was going through. Fact is, he hadn't even tried to find out. He had just left.

Steve reached for the phone. He knew it was late, but he doubted Leslie was sleeping. When he heard her voice, he simply said, "Leslie, I'm at the Sunset Hotel, but I'll be home tomorrow so we can talk. Try not to worry. Everything will somehow work out okay. You know I love you." As Leslie heard these words, she began to cry again, but this time they were a healing balm. She knew with Steve at her side everything would be okay.

Chapter 48

Mary Ann was really pleased when the results were announced, and she was named valedictorian of her class. Tonya was a close second. Joan and Paul were delighted, but not surprised. Mary Ann had always been an excellent student, never having to study that much. She was able to handle her classes and still participate in gymnastics, cheer leading, school paper activities, and anything extra that came along. She seemed to have an abundance of energy.

Mary Ann had been thinking about the speech she would have to make. The valedictory address was important, and she wanted to say just the right things. It must not be long and boring, but brief and inspiring. Papa had offered to help her, but she wanted this to be all hers, right from the heart. She wanted everyone to feel the happiness and joy that she felt and to take advantage of the remarkable opportunities that lay out there. She realized that not everyone had been as lucky as she had. No one could have had a mama and papa like hers. Even Tonya, who was happy as could be with Hannah and Peter, had had a really rough beginning. Mary Ann's life had always been beautiful, and she had always had the love and support of her parents. As Mary Ann thought about her classmates and other friends she knew, she realized that many of them had come from broken homes, poverty, and even abuse. She realized that she didn't live in a perfect world, but her beloved mama and papa had made it so for her. She wanted more than anything to please them and to be everything they wished her to be. She couldn't even imagine how life would be without them.

Graduation was only a week away, and she still had much to do. Her speech wasn't written, and she hadn't decided for sure what she would wear. She had mailed her invitations the week before, and she had reserved the seats for Mama and Papa. She wanted them to be as near the front as possible. She wanted to be able to see their faces as she spoke. There would be a big party after graduation, but she had to concentrate right now on that special speech she would make. Tonya would speak just before her. Mary Ann's would be the final speech of the evening. Then the diplomas would be handed out. Tomorrow, the seniors would practice marching. Not long now and high school would be behind her. Time had flown by. Seemed only yesterday that she cut her arm in the first grade. She automatically rubbed the scar, remembering Tonya's concern and the principal carrying her to his car. Where had the years gone? She had thought that graduation would never come, but when it did, it seemed so fast.

Mary Ann sighed a deep sigh and thought, "I'd better get busy on my speech before the time slips by." This past year had been so happy for her. She was looking forward to nursing school and was already planning on the day she would start working at Maple Memorial Hospital. She had always loved that hospital; in fact, it was where she was born. It had changed somewhat in the last few years. New wings had been added, and the old ones rejuvenated, but it was still Maple Memorial. It was there she wanted to work, taking care of her hometown's people. Some of her classmates were looking forward to big cities and a more glamorous lifestyle, but Warren had always suited her. Anyway, she wanted to be near Mama and Papa, especially as they got older. She'd be there to take care of them.

She shuddered a little and had a somewhat uneasy feeling. She had such a perfect life, it scared her sometimes. Tonya had laughed when she had mentioned this earlier to her and called her superstitious, but it really wasn't that. It was just the realization that all things aren't perfect, and up to now she felt her life had been all she could have wished for. Tonya was probably right, and she was just being silly. She was just extremely happy. There was no reason not to be.

Chapter 49

True to his word, early the next morning, Steve was home, making the coffee when Leslie got up. As soon as she came into the kitchen, Steve was there taking her in his arms, telling her over and over how sorry he was that he had acted so badly and so irresponsibly. Of course, all of this had been a big shock, but he knew he should have handled himself better. It was a shock to Leslie, too. To suddenly find out that the baby she thought had died was not dead all these years, but a live, beautiful eighteen-year-old girl. Steve wanted again to hear all about Angel, all the things Leslie knew. Together they would work out just how to go about claiming their child. Steve called the office to say he wouldn't be in today. He knew that he and Leslie needed time to put everything in perspective and to reevaluate all the evidence that pointed to Mary Ann Lambert really being Angel.

They tried to act normal when Cynthia and Patrick came in for breakfast before heading off to school. Steve couldn't take his eyes off either of them, all the time wondering what the news of a big sister would do to them. How could they ever understand what he had done to Leslie while she was still in high school? Suppose he and Leslie had not married. Would she have found him and told him he had a child? How many lives would be touched by this news? Jacob and Emily, his sister and her family, the doctors and nurses Leslie worked with, their pastor and all their church friends. What might seem like a miracle to Leslie could well be a scandal to everyone else. A baby born out of wedlock from a forced relationship and then hidden from the world when she died. What about Angel herself and the people she believed to be her parents and her friends? Would she hate them for disrupting her good life?

Leslie had fantasized about Angel running into her arms happy to be reunited with her real parents, but Angel wasn't even aware that she was not truly Mary Ann Lambert or that Joan and Paul weren't her parents at all. What kind of turmoil would this put in her life? This was a situation so bizarre that it was unbelievable. Truly it could be a nightmare.

All through the day Leslie and Steve looked at Angel's picture in the paper and went over and over every detail that they were aware of. Leslie's first impulse was to drive as fast as possible to the Lamberts' house and claim her Angel. Of course, she and Steve both knew that they could not do this—but how? With the end of school less than a week away, they knew they had to wait until after graduation. They couldn't upset "Angel" just when she was about to be honored. She was the valedictorian and would give the main student address at the graduation. Leslie didn't know how she could wait, but she knew she had to wait these few more days before being able to claim her child.

Finally, Steve and Leslie agreed they would wait, but only until graduation ceremonies were over. They would both be there at the close to share this joyous occasion with Angel, ready to claim her as their own. Steve had all kinds of misgivings, but Leslie was sure that everything would work out beautifully. It was all Leslie could do to keep from jumping in the car and racing to the school just to get a better look at their daughter. She had promised Steve, however, that she wouldn't do anything foolish, but would wait until the time was right for both of them to claim her.

Graduation day finally arrived, and while Leslie and Steve were preparing themselves for the big event, Mary Ann was very excited. She had decided to wear a simple white sheath dress under her white gown. This would look better, she thought, and the dress would be perfect for the party following graduation. She had written and rewritten her speech several times, but finally decided just to speak from her heart what the momentous occasion meant to her and her aspirations for the future. She was both happy and sad—sad to be leaving all the years of her youth behind, happy to be moving ahead into the life she had chosen for herself. Mama and Papa had seemed a little sad, too, but Mary Ann knew they were truly proud and happy for her. She had been their little girl for eighteen wonderful years, but now she had grown up.

When the time finally came, Mary Ann dressed and was all ready when Papa called to her, "Sweetheart, it's time to go." After a few smiles and hugs, Joan, Paul, and Mary Ann left for the auditorium and Mary Ann's big night.

Leslie had been dressed for hours and felt as if the time would never come. Cynthia and Patrick were going to spend the evening with Jacob, Emily, and Michael Jacob. All she had told Jacob was that she and Steve had an important engagement. Oh, how she wished she could have told him the real truth, but the time wasn't yet right. She had told Mona that they were going to see Angel tonight, but nothing more. Graduation was at 8:00 P.M., but she and Steve wanted to get there early to ensure getting good seats. They didn't want to miss a single second of Angel's big night. They arrived at the auditorium at 7:20, but by the time they had found just the right seats, it was already 7:45, and the auditorium was fast filling up. Of course, parents of the graduates had seats reserved at the very front, and Leslie felt like saying, "We should be up there." However, she was pleased that she and Steve had found seats that would allow them a good view of the graduates and especially of the speakers. She wanted to share this night with Angel as the beginning of their lives with her. Steve was still somewhat apprehensive, but nothing could dampen Leslie's spirits tonight.

Joan and Paul kissed Mary Ann as she entered through the side door, and they hurried on to the main entrance so they could take the seats their daughter had reserved for them. Never had they been so proud as they were tonight. Never had Mary Ann looked more beautiful and happy. This was indeed a joyous occasion.

The first strains of the processional started, and a hush fell over the auditorium. Doors at the back opened, and here they came, the graduates, all smiles, marching in pairs. This was their big moment. The one they had worked and waited twelve years for. Leslie and Steve watched carefully as each face passed them, searching for that one Angel face. Then there she was, more beautiful than her picture had been and no doubt theirs. The eyes, her smile, the tilt of her head, with the golden hair falling from beneath the cap. Even the way she walked was so like Leslie. A lump swelled in her throat, and tears escaped from her eyes as Leslie held tightly to Steve's hand. He, too, was filled with emotion and a surge of pride as he watched his daughter pass by. If only she could know they were there, but then she would know when the ceremonies were over. They would be waiting for her.

As in a daze, Leslie and Steve watched and listened as the superintendent spoke, then introduced the salutatorian,

Tonya Magness, and then the main speaker, Dr. Hightower, from the nearby college. After they had both spoken, the superintendent stepped up to the podium to introduce the last speaker, and the valedictorian of the graduating class, Mary Ann Lambert. All the classmates and the people applauded—the room was packed—as Mary Ann stepped forward. Leslie felt faint as Mary Ann began to speak. "Parents, teachers, friends, and classmates. It is my great honor to address you here tonight. My greatest honor, however, is to have known you, to have studied with you, laughed with you, and cried with you during the past twelve years. We have been bound together by an unseen thread, and in the years to come we will look back on these times and remember how good they were and how beautiful life can be. Each of us has charted a new course and new paths to follow—some to college and beginnings of careers. Others will be joining the military, and still others will be going into business or into the time-honored role of homemakers. Whatever your endeavors, never forget the lessons of honesty, fair play, and love that you have learned on a daily basis here at Warren High. Our principal and our teachers have instilled in us those qualities that we will need in following our careers and in living every day in this world. To them, we say thank you from the bottom of our hearts for your time and deep concerns for our well-being. We owe you a great debt. To all of you parents and friends who have molded our lives, we shall be eternally grateful.

"For myself, I would like to say that the two greatest people on this earth are my parents, Joan and Paul Lambert. They have guided my footsteps from the day I was born. When I stumbled, they were there to pick me up. When I was ill, they were there to bathe my brow. They have counseled me when I've been sad or troubled, and they have rejoiced with me when I've been happy. Whatever I am or ever hope to be, I clearly owe to my mama and papa. I truly believe God has a hand in choosing your parents, and he gave me the best. As we leave this building and say goodbye forever to these walls of learning, I say farewell to all my classmates. May God go with you and provide the light that leads you."

One by one diplomas were handed out, awards given, and the ceremonies were over. Leslie never heard a word.

Amid applause and whistles, the recessional started as the happy graduates eagerly began their new journeys. Leslie and Steve stood with the audience, tears running down their faces. They watched as that now-familiar figure passed in front of them. A happy smile of expectation was on her face.

As the music concluded and the people began to rush out, Leslie clutched Steve's hand, and with a small sad smile, she said, "Steve, our Angel died eighteen years ago. Let's go home to Cynthia and Patrick."